by Steve Katz

CREAMY AND DELICIOUS

CREAMY AND DELICIOUS

EAT MY WORDS (in Other Words)

STEVE KATZ

ILLUSTRATED BY RICHARD TUM SUDEN

TOUGH POETS PRESS | ARLINGTON, MASSACHUSETTS

Some of these stories first appeared
in *Epoch*, *US #1*, *Get That*, and
Kumquat. The following stories first
appeared in *Extensions*: "Mythology: *Diana*"
and "Mythology: *Hermes*."

ISBN 978-0-578-28764-5

www.toughpoets.com

TO

AVRUM,

NIKOLAI,

AND

RAFAEL

CREAMY AND DELICIOUS

EAT MY WORDS (in other words)

3 SATISFYING STORIES

3 SATISFYING STORIES

H

At first she believed that she herself had volunteered some-where to make this trip, but now she realized that wasn't the case. She had been sent. It wasn't a place she would decide to stay in, as frivolous as she sometimes got. This was a different place. She noticed that everything was built up of yellow stone that crumbled and made the streets yellow. It was surrounded on three sides by the bare ridges of a dry canyon that opened onto sand dunes to the South. The room she had been given was unfurnished, the walls unplastered, made of the same powdery yellow stone, that yellowed her clothes as she laid them out on the floor. There was no closet, she had no newspa-per, and there was no one to ask for anything, only the children below in the courtyard—if you could call the bare compound where the children sat around in some kind of desolate stupor a courtyard. She realized she would have to contrive for herself a bed out of the wardrobe she had carefully selected for her excursion. That gave her a certain feeling of exhilaration.

She had been sent, she was sure, to do something, but she hadn't been told what it was, nor did she expect to be. Out her window she noticed some water oozing from a fountain in one corner of the compound, and after she arranged her books against the wall by her bed she went out to have a drink. The children were gone, perhaps to their beds, since it was so hot. The dull golden glow from the stone made it hotter than it was, which was hotter than she could imagine. The fountain had nearly stopped, though she could see that what little flowed there was as clear as water, or clearer, but heavier, like mineral oil. There was no vegetation near the fountain, nor anywhere else nearby, except on the ridges where she could make out some spare patches of brush. It was the water. She tasted it, and the oily texture it left on her palate never quit her mouth for as long as she rested in that place. She returned to her room and noticed that her books were gone.

What she had to do, she decided, was to teach in that place, to teach the children. She had never done that before and the idea delighted her somewhat, though she didn't understand the language of the children, didn't know what language it was, and she noted, in fact, that the children rarely spoke at all. They were a sullen lot of kids, more like prisoners, and they never played, and were never joyous like the children she had always known from where she once lived. The extent of her problem gave her courage and energy, though the soup and bread that was left twice a day at her door wasn't enough food to keep her healthy. She became so immediately involved in the problem of the children that she never got curious to know who brought the soup. They weren't easy children to teach, and there were no conditions for teaching. The room she used was bare and yellow like all the rest,—no desks, no blackboards, no books. She was overjoyed when she discovered that she could write on the wall by moistening a stiff roll of denim she made from a pocket of her jeans. The problem was not getting the children to sit still. They were used to it; but it was difficult to make them understand what it meant to learn. They sat there receiving nothing, like statues. Indeed they looked like statues, they were all so thickly covered with the yellow dust of the place.

She concluded that she would have to teach them first to play. Her inability to communicate with them was sustained by the lack of communication amongst themselves. But she found no easy way to teach them games. Hopscotch was no use. Three-legged races were incommunicable. They weren't curious enough about one another to learn hide and seek. She needed a ball. A ball would make them want to catch it, and was nice because you could kick it. A ball was good because they could throw it back and forth, from one little child to the other.

She was inspired that evening when lying in her bed and her hand brushed what used to be the raincoat. The plastic raincoat could do it. She stayed up all night fashioning balls from pieces of her raincoat, blowing them up and tying off the ends with rope she braided of her long red hair. A few she stuffed with rags and dust to give them heft, and by morning she had seven delightful playthings. She threw three out her window and rushed into the yard with the other four. The children sat about indifferently petrified as she rushed around tossing, kicking, catching the balls. She was delirious with laughter at her success in making them, but the children wouldn't even look at her. Their dark eyes focused, as always, on nothing, and some of the eyes were closed. Slowly her enthusiasm turned to weariness and she went to her room, stretched out on her yellowed heap of clothes, and fell asleep before she could even weep.

She woke up thinking she must have been somewhere else because there was noise from the courtyard of joyful children. She rushed to the window and saw them playing there. They were playing. She had never known before how happy she could be. They were playing a game like baseball, they had invented a kind of soccer, and there was a primitive sort of basketball at one end. Her mind boggled at the speed at which it had happened. Some of them were laughing. She had never heard them laugh before and it made her cry. She wanted to be able to speak with somebody about her success. Her watch, which she had preserved, said ten minutes to twelve. At twelve promptly every day her soup and bread were at the door. Somebody brought it there. Who? It made no difference. In order to catch whoever it was and lead him to the window to show off her success she waited by the door, but the food didn't come that noon, nor did it come in the evening when she waited again. It would come, she discovered, only when she was out of sight, and only at the accustomed hour. In order to have someone to speak with she would have to teach the children her language.

It had been some time since she thought of anything but her work with the children, when she saw the dust in the distance of someone approaching. She saw it first, and then the children saw it. She was suddenly frightened to realize she was there and didn't know what was to become of her. Had she really volunteered to come to this place? No. She had been sent. The children rushed to her door in excitement when they saw the dust coming, and she calmed them, saying words that left her mouth from nowhere. "Don't worry children. It's the governor. The governor is coming." She herself was surprised by that announcement, and rushed to the fountain to wash.

When the governor arrived with his small entourage of men, she had the children lined up in somewhat unruly ranks because along with everything she taught them they had lost their ability to keep still. At first the governor seemed not to notice her. He twisted slowly in his saddle, looking around. He was an immense man, tall and round, of a weight that would seem a burden for two horses. He wore a tall sheepskin hat and his bulk was draped in lengths of fine pale blue cotton, beneath which he wore black silk pants with mauve stripes. He seemed annoyed at the children and said something to his men in an unidentifiable language. She approached his saddle and looked up at him. He didn't frighten her, but she saw no kindness in his face.

"Welcome, Governor," she said.

"What have you been doing here?" he asked. She had heard the accent before but couldn't place it.

"I should be very pleased to show you what I have been doing."

As the governor dismounted she noticed in his saddle that was decorated with fragments of mirror that her face, though she had washed it, was as yellow as the faces of her children, permanently stained over a skin she had once been vain of for its whiteness and softness. The governor's face was pale.

"Governor," she said, "though you perhaps notice less discipline in the children than previous to my arrival, I think you will find that generally their condition is improved. I have been teaching them my language, and they are doing well. They are also learning to use numbers, and to sing." She led him into a small room where she taught geography. "Here I have tried to carve a map of the world as far as I can remember it, and I have explained to them where places are in the world, though they have no idea, nor do I, where this one is." She could see, by how quickly the governor turned away, that he didn't feel obliged to answer the question she had implied.

"Governor," she said. "We have made a great deal of progress here since I came. The children have come alive and are learning swiftly. I don't speak out of vanity when I say that I think I am doing some good here, though I can't tell why. If it is not too much of a luxury to ask I should like to request some materials to help me in this work. A pencil—one would be enough for now. A few pieces of paper. I told the children about paper and they didn't understand. I don't mind it here, you see. There is some satisfaction in it."

The huge governor rotated away from her and walked back to his horse. Four men helped him to mount.

"Governor," she pleaded, approaching his saddle. "Your reply."

"In thirty days all children here must die." He didn't look at her when he spoke.

She burst into laughter when she heard him. "Governor," she said. "Please be serious. What did you say?"

He turned his horse. "In thirty days all the children here must die." He rode off.

At first she behaved as if she didn't understand what he had said, or as if it couldn't be true. She kept the children in their routine and laughed to herself about the governor's visit. She looked up frequently at the direction in which he had disappeared. When she finally went to her room to rest, and looked out the window at the strange, yellowed children, and then at her own changed flesh she realized that he must have been sincere. He must have intended the children to die in thirty days. She folded her arms across her belly and began to cry. "What am I doing in this place?" she repeated over and over. She knew now that she hadn't volunteered, or if she had volunteered it wasn't to come to this place. She had been sent. He meant it. The governor meant to kill all the children in her compound. If that was the case, had she mistaken her job? Had she been sent to teach? Why would he decide to kill them just when they had begun to make progress? What was she supposed to do in that place? Why had they given her no assignment? Was the weight she felt responsibility? What was she doing there?

Late that night she realized that she must prevent the governor from killing children, even at the expense of her own life. Even to let them take their own lives would be better. She had to give them a chance to escape, even if that meant letting them die on their own. That would be better, surely, than to be slaughtered in who knows what fashion at the governor's whim. They would die free, she thought.

From the next day till the day of the governor's return she put aside her bread, dipping it in the soup so it would soak up nutrition, and letting it dry. She assembled the children in groups of five, told them of what was to come, and advised them to get away into the mountains or into the desert. They took her advice, because everything else she had taught them had been delightful, and therefore they esteemed her so. Each evening five of them left, taking her bread and a bit of their own food. There were wolves in the mountains, and the desert was the desert, but she reassured them and sent them off in good spirits. On the day the governor was to return only she was left and one lame, half-witted child she was determined to defend with her own body. She washed at the fountain and found herself so weak she could hardly move away, but fell into a strange, wakeful slumber of dreams and vague vegetable forms.

She was awakened by the governor who had arrived this time with an entourage of more than twenty men on horseback, all bearing gifts. "Where are the children?" asked the governor. She immediately looked around for her lame, half-witted boy but saw him held on the saddle by one of the men, laughing and playing with his braid.

"Where are the children?" the governor asked again.

She rose up stiff as a martyr and looked into the governor's eyes. "I made them go away. I made them leave by the mountains or the desert because I wouldn't have them killed by you."

"Foolish woman," the governor said. "There are wolves in

the mountains and in the desert there is heat and they will die of thirst."

"We decided that was better than to let you slaughter them."

"Slaughter them? Look to your own hands. You have killed them, woman. You should have known I was jesting with your patience, and if you had patience you would have known it. As you can see, I brought them gifts."

At a signal from the governor his entourage dismounted and laid the packages on the ground. The remaining boy slowly began to unwrap his gift and mumble. It was a music box in the shape of a phonograph. When he lifted the cover it played "La Marseillaise." He was delighted.

"There, woman," said the governor, as he wheeled his horse about, the shadow of his hugeness passing over her for a moment like cool hands. "There is the result of your foolishness." He gestured at the half-wit, and at the empty courtyard.

It surprised her after the governor had left her with the little boy that she didn't regret what she had done. That was the way it had happened. How could it have happened differently? The governor was right. She had interfered and was liable for that, but she hadn't volunteered to come to this place. She had been sent. Could it have happened differently? She had certainly made the best decisions. She looked at her mat of yellowed clothes and thought of beating them clean, as if it was time to pack and leave.

The governor hadn't been gone two hours when the half-wit's music box exploded, spattering her with blood and flesh and bone. All the other boxes exploded too, almost simultaneously. She held her box tightly and spoke to it saying, "Explode. Explode." She was curious of how it would feel. It wouldn't explode. She unwrapped it hastily and found a music box inside in the shape of a phonograph. When she lifted the lid it played "America the Beautiful." It wouldn't explode.

She could volunteer to leave but she knew she would have to be sent away. A knock on the door preceded the entrance of a blind old man carrying her soup and bread.

"Why do you cry?" he asked.

"I'm not crying, sir; but I'm unhappy," she replied.

"You needn't cry, you can have anything you ask for," he said gently, stroking her face with his fingertips.

"I should like to bathe," she said. "It's been forever since I had a bath."

U

"Why do you cry?" he asked.

"I'm not crying, sir; but I'm unhappy," she replied.

"You needn't cry, you can have anything you ask for," he said gently, stroking her face with his fingertips.

"I should like to bathe," she said. "It's been forever since I had a bath."

She didn't know why she had made that request. It was absurd. She had just bathed, and her habits of personal hygiene were no less than impeccable. Perhaps it was because he had offered her anything, and she wanted nothing, except to feel more cheerful. The situation in which she found herself was so peculiar.

"Certainly that too is possible." He led her by the arm to the washroom. "You can shower here if you like and even change clothes. There are clothes your size hanging in the wardrobe. Perhaps you can find something that will better suit your red hair." He left. She thought it wasn't his place to criticize her taste in clothes, though she would admit she had a fondness for the dress she was wearing, despite the fact that her red hair was lost in its shade of rose.

She found in the wardrobe one lovely brocade that she slipped on, and dressed thus she stepped into the crowded salon where the party was already underway. At one end was the bar and conversation, at the other end the band and dancing. She went immediately to the other end where she began to dance with a man dressed in blue. It was smoky there. People were tossing colored streamers across the dance floor so they lit on the heads and shoulders of the dancers. It was a festivity of the most general sort that everyone celebrated with noisemakers, whistles and toy pistols. They were dressed in elegant perfect suits, in stained denims and sandals, in bells and robes. She felt an exhilaration from the dancing, and wanted to say that she was happy. She was. Between the first and the second dance her partner asked where she came from. Between the third and fourth he asked her what she did. From time to time they said to each other, "Soul, baby" while they danced. The dress she had borrowed held a new coolness around her body and she moved inside it with strange buoyancy. Around her the people danced beautifully, easily, and made her dance as if motionless, the only movement being of the music that was within her. The band played as if it had never begun and would never end. In the room adjacent where a TV was shining without sound, people lounged about, smoking. It amused her to see them, how smoking put them at ease, and how soft and friendly their speech was. She liked to smoke, but she never did. That was her habit. On the dance floor the people had begun to play a game with balls, passing them back and forth. They used seven balls in all that frequently struck each other in midair, causing an infectious uproar of laughter. She started to kick and toss the balls herself and couldn't remember ever before having been so happy, though she didn't know where she was, nor how she had got there, but the people did begin to seem familiar. When she was exhausted she turned her attention to the other end of the salon where there was drinking and conversation. Wherever she had lived before was among such people, but they didn't dance so easily on the one hand, nor on the other hand did they have so much to say to each other.

". . . feel that last time it was better. More action-packed. This time it all seems a little timid. I don't know. Of course we always recall the past in such a way that it glows. It's impossible, you know, to compare what is happening now, what you're doing at a given moment, to an experience that memory has worked over. Maybe one time was just different from another, and you can't evaluate. Or maybe that time wasn't actually so good as I like to remember it, and this time is better, because I'm enjoying myself more now just by reason of this conversation. I take pleasure in talking to you about how much I enjoyed myself last time, whether I actually enjoyed it or not. I say I had a better time because saying makes it better, though we can't go back, can we? It's like relativity."

"Pleasure has always been a confusing issue."

"And I am enjoying talking to you."

It was delightful to overhear elegant talk. The woman was tall, her body curved like a longbow, and the man with whom she spoke was bald. She passed to another group, centered about a bearded man seated on a couch, discussing his travels with a group of admirers.

"I saw Jerry, Lynn and Dodge in Benares. It was hot. Those English girls were in Kabul."

"You didn't buy a coat, did you?"

"No, but Chuck did, one of the long yellow ones with long sleeves and red tattooing, or whatever you call that stuff. I met Jethro in Katmandu, strung out on Meth of course—but Toby was still with him, and Fluff was with her as usual. Nepal is a gas. Everybody's there and everybody's stoned. The Afghans are groovy too because they smoke all the time, and they're all stoned, everyone, the shepherds, the cops. The only place that wasn't so groovy, especially because I was with a chick, was Iran. Wow. In Tehran they spit on my chick. They're fierce, man. And Istanbul. Man people get busted there, chicks disappear, wow . . ."

At that point a man took her arm and began conversing with her alone as he led her to the table from which drinks were served. He spoke so fast she couldn't understand him, and she couldn't imagine that anyone would talk that fast. It was as if something was going to happen soon. The noise in the room had risen almost an octave, as if everyone at once began to speak faster in order to get it all in. It had never happened that way where she was from, even among the brightest conversationalists. The man led her to a book-shelf, talking even faster, and began to take books off the shelf, examining them, and leaving some in her hands, until she had three books. "What time is it?" he said suddenly and dis-tinctly.

"It's ten to twelve," said almost everyone in the room. The conversation resumed a pace again that she could understand. She was in the midst of young men dressed casual but clean. They spoke with energy.

"I still believe that if a child takes his first breath of air he is alive and to kill him is murder. It's a sin. That's where I draw the line, at the first breath," said the one with the ascot.

"Don't you see that your upbringing is a hang-up of cul-tural conditioning that leads to your opinion. It's not your thought that you express, it's your training. When I say that I believe in infanticide I mean that we need a rational response to the population problem. I believe in infanticide."

"You can't. You can't just sacrifice humanity on the altar of rationality. Your solution is too simple. People are involved . . ."

"You see, you still believe in the sanctity of human life. You still believe that, even though you're alive in the twentieth century with concentration camps, purges, pogroms, Vietnam. You believe in the sanctity of human life. You believe in the sanctity of human life. You believe in the sanctity of human life." His voice slowly ground to a halt as the clock struck noon. The room had become suddenly silent. She thought they were waiting for the clock to finish striking before they spoke again, but that wasn't the case. Everyone was rigid. She touched the man who had just been speaking because his vigor had pleased her, but he was like a signpost. Everything had stopped. People froze in mid-sentence, frozen with drinks halfway to their lips, frozen fingering their noses, their ears, frozen bored, frozen laughing. She found it remarkable that such a thing could happen, even in a situation that was as totally strange to her as this one. The dance floor was full of grotesques, because the gestures people had been caught in weren't graceful. They were twisted like wrung clothes; those who had been jumping were caught off the ground, held as if by levitation. What was strangest for her was that she was conscious and could move. She assumed that if she had been frozen she would know nothing of it. The state they were in seemed familiar to her, as if she had dreamed about it once, or had been there, but she had never been so differentiated from them. The seven balls had stopped in mid air and hung like a constellation above the still dancers. The people in the room adjacent seemed caught in a kind of smoky gelatin. They were smiling or raising their eyelids. She noticed in a mirror that she too was smiling, though she didn't know why.

She was surprised to be able to open the door and step out into the adjoining corridor. The few people who had been passing through at noon had remained there, rigid. The elevator was stopped between floors so she hurried down the stairs that seemed endless, winding around the elevator shaft for story on story till she was dizzy when she reached the bottom, but the silence in the street was sobering. Not a sound. Not one of the layers of noise that made the city was left. Cars stopped. Jetliners held in the sky. People caught running in midstreet. The rigidity was general all over the city.

Then she heard the sound of a brush sweeping the pavement. That's what it was, a man in brown uniform pushing a cart full of brooms and cleaning the street. She ran to him as if he were her father.

"Why don't I understand what's happening here?" she asked him. He didn't speak until she repeated the question three times.

"One must keep the place clean. I circulate at this time to clean the whole works." She knew by his tone that he would say nothing else, as if it should have been obvious to her what the "whole works" was.

She suddenly became aware of the heft of the three books under her arm and looked at them for the first time. One was called *Animals Without Backbones*, another was Volume Two of Boswell's *The Life of Samuel Johnson* and the third was a selection from the Burton translation of *The Arabian Nights*. She sat down on a bench opposite the Governor's mansion to read, and found the first of the books to be empty, for the print had been taken away. It was true of the second and the third. The books were gone. It occurred to her at that moment that she was dead. There could be no other answer to the questions these unusual circumstances raised. If she were otherwise than dead there would be some clue. The discovery made her happy. It was easier that way, to know that she wasn't just alive in some extraordinary predicament. This was death, then, and it wasn't so very bad. She crossed the street to the Governor's mansion and went in past the rigid guards and receptionist. The Governor was huge and pale and sat still. She sat opposite him in a chair and watched him for a while until she decided the interview was over. She rose and shook his hand, but when she twisted it slightly the hand came off, and the yellow dust which filled out the Governor's bulk poured out of the arm, covering the desk top, swirling up into the air. She left the Governor's mansion and headed across the street to the hospital. She had never understood that death could be such pleasant isolation, for she wasn't lonely, but she was alone.

She entered the hospital through the staff entrance and they stopped her at the desk.

"Did you volunteer to come here?" asked the receptionist as a matter of routine.

"No. I was sent," she said.

"We need help today in the maternity ward," she was told.

She took a uniform, stole a scalpel, showered, dressed and went to the maternity ward where she immediately began to bathe and change the babies. There were thousands of them, and it made her giddy to think about it with the special knowledge she now had. She settled on one that she was asked to take to its mother and was surprised to find the little thing warm as she carried it in blankets, cradled in her arms. The mother lay still weak in her bed. When she entered she showed the mother the baby and then began to undress it. "Now watch," she said to the mother after the baby was completely naked.

She plunged the scalpel into the throat of the baby and swiftly slit it down through the belly. To her surprise the baby bled, covering her with warm blood and intestine. She put the finished infant down by its mother and stepped into the corridor where she started to walk slowly away. When the doctor caught up with her he didn't say a word. The doctor motioned for her to sit down on a nearby bench and made another sign she took to mean she must remain there. She sat quietly with her hands folded in her lap and thought about what had happened. It wasn't clear.

B

The doctor motioned for her to sit down on a nearby bench and made another sign that she took to mean she must remain there. She sat quietly with her hands folded in her lap and thought about what had happened. It wasn't clear. She was there, on board, and that was that. She called the man who had led her to her seat "the doctor" because he was dressed like one and had a stethoscope hung from his neck. He was the ship's doctor; she thought. It was a strange ship because it had left port under some kind of power but once at sea it spread sail like a schooner, on masts she hadn't noticed before. She was pleased at the idea of a voyage, but would have appreciated knowing her destination. What could have happened to her? She could remember none of the recent past, but kept recalling a trivial incident from several years earlier when she was visiting the Colosseum in Rome and slugged a man with her handbag who had been pestering her all day. He bled. That was irrelevant, though it kept coming back. What she wanted to remember was that moment when she must have joyfully elected to make this voyage. It amused her that she couldn't. She noticed that she was sitting in a small, wood-paneled anteroom before what must have been the door to the Captain's quarters, though the noise from within sounded like a kitchen. She had been left alone for quite some time and tried to speculate about what they were preparing within. She couldn't. She recalled that no one had said anything to her since she got on the ship, and they had just been whispering to each other, as if they didn't want her to understand the language. She was curious about the language.

When the doors opened she discovered that the room wasn't the Captain's quarters as she had suspected, but was some kind of elaborately equipped operating theatre. The decor was sumptuous, however, the floor covered with carpets, and the walls with lushly textured paper. On one wall was a picture of the Governor in his youth, on horseback. He was huge and pale. She was directed to remove her shoes before stepping on the carpets.

The Captain was there, and he greeted her in a language that to her dismay she couldn't recognize. He was attentive of her long red hair, which he stroked as if it were fine fur. She noticed then that everyone on the ship was blonde, though they all had dark eyes. The Captain, after begging her permission, clipped a long lock of the hair to save for himself. When the doctor appeared she appealed to him as a man of learning, complimenting him on the fine equipment he had, and finally saying, "If I am not being presumptuous, I should appreciate your explaining the nature of my predicament."

At first she noted a look on his face like a clear light and she thought he had caught on, but apparently he didn't understand her language either, because after regarding her for a moment he turned and left. She found herself alone in the room. Medical equipment always seemed ominous to her but she dismissed that old feeling because there was nothing to fear here; she was being treated well. Up on deck the sailors off duty were kicking a ball around. She leaned on the bridge rail and watched them. She had never seen so many dark-eyed blond-haired men at play. When they spotted her they began to entertain her, competing more strenuously, heading the ball, lofting it with the back of the foot. She cheered. Unfortunately the outcome was that too often a strong kick sent a ball flying into the sea. They lost seven in all while she was watching, and when they quit she watched the seven balls bob in the sea as if they were alive.

She had complete freedom of the ship except for the hour or more she was constrained to spend with the doctor in the medical room each day. Though her quarters were pleasant, indeed luxurious, she preferred to stay out on deck because the sea was calm, the air refreshing, and the sun healthful. The doctor listened at her belly each day with his stethoscope, and probed her sexual parts, not lasciviously, but clinically. It amused her that she was being treated as a pregnant woman, because there was no chance of that, but the doctor was satisfied with whatever progress he thought she made. When her period came once, twice, even a third time she couldn't even toy with the idea any more that she was pregnant, not even a remote chance, though the doctor still seemed satisfied with her condition. Perhaps it was something else he was looking after.

When the Captain came to her cabin the first time to take her away to make love she was pleased. She liked to make love, because she was beautiful, and her days at sea had made that beauty flourish. The Captain, who was an older man, admired her. She liked to be admired for her small hands and her slender grace. He was a strong lover, robust but gentle, and she liked to touch his weathered skin. They didn't go to his cabin to make love, but down to the hold, where he had another bed, and they would stay there for several hours, fondling each other among the sealed barrels. She often wondered what was in the barrels.

Once on the Captain's locked shelves she noticed what looked like a five-volume picture encyclopedia. He obligingly took the volumes down and let her look at them. She opened it at random to a picture of a strange town. The words of the language looked almost impossible to pronounce, thick with consonants, some of them written in another letter system. She thought it would be interesting to have the five books for a while so she could attempt an inroad on the language, but when they came back to the cabin from the hold the books were gone. The language was impossible. Over a period of five months, which she reckoned by her menstruation, two of which she had been intimate with the Captain, she couldn't speak the simplest sentence. Even his word for making love changed every time, as did his approach. When she tried to repeat a phrase she remembered hearing the previous day no one understood her. The language seemed to change itself from day to day, perhaps from hour to hour. That was one frustrating thing; otherwise the people were industrious, affable and kind. She noticed in the Captain's mirror that she was getting more beautiful among them. How lucky she was to be voyaging.

Whatever strangeness she felt in her belly she thought was a reaction to the constant attention of the doctor, who was making her feel pregnant against her better knowledge. Her belly was flat as usual, and she was in wonderful condition, exercising every day, but still she found herself frequently sitting or standing with her arms folded over her belly like a pregnant woman, as if there were something alive inside.

She would have liked to ask the Captain about it because she knew she could converse nicely with him if she only had the language. That was the sort of small intimacy they had in love. One morning when he came to get her unusually early she decided she would try to ask him what they expected of her, working it out with gestures. After they made love she leaned back against a barrel and began the impossible work of communication. The Captain watched her silently, nodding as if he understood what she wanted. He had understood something. Obviously he took her large, round gestures to mean she was curious about the barrels. She was curious about the barrels, and therefore didn't try to correct him when he got some tools and went to break one open. That would be one further question she wouldn't have to ask.

The barrels were full of yellow dust that caught on every slight air-current and swirled up into the hold. For the first time she was frightened. The Captain looked up from his operation on the second barrel and said suddenly, "It's ten to twelve." The sound of her own language made her cry. Why hadn't he let her know that he could speak it? Everything she had presumed was mistaken, and she was in danger. She passed suddenly into a yellow stupor.

She was in the operating room surrounded by technicians. Her top half was covered with sheets, but her lower was exposed. What they expected of her was to give birth. How could she? There wasn't the slightest swelling in her, and her period had come religiously for the past nine months on the ship. She didn't feel one contraction of labor pains. They watched her carefully under the antiseptic lights. "I can't," she screamed. "It's impossible." A technician took her hand to comfort her, and another cupped her face in the anesthetist's mask. "It's twelve o'clock," he said.

A nurse attended her in the recuperation room. Had she given birth? She felt a motherly pang and her midsection was weak as if all the muscles had been spent. The nurse unbuttoned her pajama and applied a breast pump. She had plenty of milk and didn't know if she should be happy about it or not. Such a thing had never happened to her before, and it was curious. Many people, including the Captain and the doctor, were crowded at the window and smiling. She too was smiling, she noticed in the mirror by her bed table, like a new mother. Perhaps they were going to bring her baby soon, if that was it. She straightened her hair. It felt dry. One of the technicians came in with something wrapped in blankets, and handed it to her. When she first unwrapped it it frightened her, grayish-pink as it was, with a whitish belly, and it was moist all over. Its eyes, on either side of its head, weren't yet open. It had no neck, flippers for arms, and a finny little tail. Its toothless snout protruded like a beak. What was it? She knew its name, but couldn't remember it in her own language.

"Burmurdouscak," said a nurse.

Its streamlined shape probably accounted for the ease of her delivery. The Captain, the doctor, the sailors, everyone all along had expected this to happen, and here she had thought she had somehow got herself into this pinch. They had been in charge. When the Captain came in she remembered that she had caught him speaking her language and she asked, "What is my child?" the "my child" sounding peculiar to her.

"Burmurdouscak," he said.

"What is it in my language? I can't remember its name."

"Burmurdouscak," he repeated.

She could feel the ship rolling now with the swells. She was at sea, and was beginning to understand why. The nurses helped her sit higher and indicated it was time for her to give the breast to her creature. She felt a little tender toward it for it was helpless as an infant, and she lifted the flap of her pajama. The hard little nose touched her nipple and she said almost immediately, "Dolphin." She remembered. That was it. She had borne a dolphin. Now she had it straight. At first she believed that she herself had volunteered somewhere to make this trip, but now she realized that wasn't the case. She had been sent.

CHAPTER 18

Are you kidding? The door to
the darkroom is always open.
Come watch him trap me.

(continued on page 43) 25

5 MYTHOLOGIES

MYTHOLOGY: FAUST

Don't believe any of those stories you had to read in college about Faust, the big scientist who wanted to know all the shit in the world, so he turned on with the devil. Don't believe all that. It's a big put-on, and maybe some of it is almost true, but none of it is really true, and if you fall for it you deserve to be pasted up on the wall like a wallpaper pattern. This here, what I'm going to lay out for you, is the real truth, the whole, and nothing but the truth, so help me. This is the story about Faust, and how he loved the girls better than he loved his homestead, and how he plowed the former deeper than he did the latter. All those other stories about him were made up, believe me, just so a bunch of professors could grunt and squeeze out the long words about him and lean around at parties and be influential; but this is the real scoop. Here comes the truth: That Faust loved the girls better than he loved his daily chores. You don't need to agonize over this. We'll just take a look at Faust out there in the field ready to hitch his mule up to a plow, a simple farmer after all, and he wanted to sock in some soy beans, some sweet potatoes and some Swiss chard. Suddenly along comes Lulu, the ravishing beauty, the daughter of the local minister, whom everybody on the block wanted a piece of but they were all afraid because the local minister put them uptight.

"Lulu," said Faust. "Step down here in my field and we'll plow up some loam."

"Socko," Lulu retorted, and she pranced down into the foamy earth with the little cheeks of her butt wobbling like tapioca.

"Oh Lulu," Faust cheered, spreading his arms and describing a mysterious figure eight with the point of his chin. His mule sat down and closed one eye. "Oh Lulu, you are the most luscious piece of tail on the block, and even though you are the minister's daughter you make all the guys horny. Me too. So now I'm going to have you for sure. Have at you. Fuck you. Ball you. Screw you. Stick you. Pump you. Lap you up. Slobber your squiff. Munch your pubes. Slurp your twat squilch. I'm going to make love to you. I'm going to sleep with you here and now." He lowered his arms, smiled like a martyr, and stroked the soft nose of his mule.

Lulu nearly blushed. "Sir," she said, "My guess is that you won't." She sighed and burbled. "But sir, if you will. Yes you will. You will. Please don't. Just don't. No. I can't. Oh, yes, yes. Stop it. No. You mustn't. Yes. Do it. Harder. No. Don't hurt me. I shouldn't. Yes. Come on. Slip it in. All the way. Stop. Not here. Ooooh. You can't do that to a girl like me. My father. Yes. Ohhhhh. Don't quit. Fuck me, Jehoshaphat. Fuck. Fuck. Can't. Now Stop. Now. Now. Don't be naughty. Yes, be naughty. Ram it into my heart. I can't. What will they think of me. Think of me. Fuck me. Put it right there and work out. Smooth. Oooohhhhh. Did I come?"

"Hold it Lulu, baby. Cool it. Don't talk yourself into anything you don't want to do. But if you're going to talk yourself into it, stop talking, and let's do it, because here's the man." And he revealed himself unto her an enormous erection like the forearm of Abraham.

"Oh my God," she exclaimed. "My God what a gorgeous thing." She fell to her knees, unhinged her lower jaw like a snake, and gobbled it, honking through her nose like a gratified mare. Faust tipped her back into the loam and fingered the flower meat she unfolded, and with her forefingers she spread the pulsing pubic petals and pulled his petzl pussywards. The mule lay down on its side. They scraunched around in the dark fertile soil till they were slicked over with a nice film of muddy sweat.

"Well," she smiled and shuddered. "That's over. Now I hope I'll see you at the services this Sunday."

"No ma'am," he said. "Not this Faust. Not if you know my story. I've got my farm to farm." He took his last gawk at the soft, moist, swollen, pink swamp-flower lips that pulsed and pullulated and gushed juice like a busted persimmon, and then he slapped his mule so it yawned and rose, and he ended the pause in his plowing. Several moments of good sun and healthy work ensued, that anyone who has ever plowed barefoot behind a mule on a warm spring day after a rain will appreciate. Suddenly another female form appeared on the horizon and when the mule recognized her he lay down immediately. It was Maggie, and she was another story entirely.

"Hi there, Faustie, you old honey-scrotum, you barrel of nuts, you insatiable cumsack."

"Why, hello, Margaret," said Faust, taken slightly aback.

"Today I've had Edgar and Zeke and Isor and Dick

and Mike and Alfred and Edsel and Floyd, and now I'm here to have you, because you're the best of them all, Faustie. Without a doubt." At that moment she slipped out of her shift and stood there naked in midfield. She was covered with grunge from head to toe.

The sight of such a befouled beauty made Faust frantic at his fly. It was an emotional experience of the first order. "Bend over Margaret," he entreated, "and touch your toes while I toddle over with my tool." His implement stretched out before him in a slender spine as straight as a rung of the ladder of Jacob. He palmed her pelvic outcroppings and patiently worked it in the neat and narrow passage. She wiggled and she giggled and she wriggled and kicked up her heels and flipped him over her back, and then she went over him and he over her in and out without missing a stroke in a wide circle like a couple of professionals.

"You do it dirty and you do it devilish," said Maggie. "But you do it good, and I've got to hand it to you." She jounced his oysters gently with her sweet fingertips.

"Madame, to service you is my greatest pleasure." Faust bowed and dismissed Maggie with a kiss on her hand.

It was later and the mule yawned and got up, and Faust ended the pause in his plowing. Several moments of good sun and healthful work ensued that anyone who has ever balled two women and then plowed barefoot behind a mule on a warm spring day after a rain will understand. Just then the long shadow of a voluptuous stranger fell across the traces and the mule stopped.

Of course you know how the story goes by now. It just keeps on telling the truth about Faust until it stops. It is a bitch to really tell the truth about Faust, as you can guess. Even this story fudges a little bit. Faust couldn't have got his farm farmed ever if he carried on like this, even if he farmed like the devil. You can't seem to say anything about Faust without lying a little, he was so extraordinary, whatever he was. He wasn't a farmer, that's for sure, but he wasn't a college professor either, and that's the truth. He was a something or other. It's hard to tell.

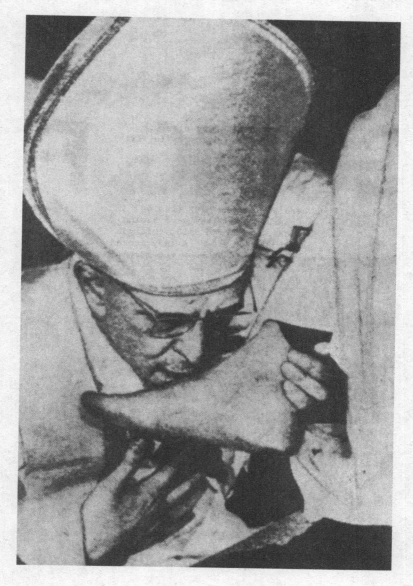

CHAPTER 6

Can a man hounded by pleasure
ever sip on the ducts of felicity?

There was the Ku Klux Klan on
the park mall. They were having
a picnic. One man said, "Did you
get those skewers?" A lady looked
up. "Yes, but somehow too much
dill."

Baffling, but it had about itself a
light, forceful, mysterious foppish-
ness, like the sneeze of a flagellant.
R added yeast and I flocked, when
someone whispered, "Times out."

 (continued on page 43)

MYTHOLOGY: DIANA

"Because Diana was the huntress, not the temptress," I replied. I forget what the question was. Anyway the ball on the 43-yard line in their own territory, fourth down, two yards to go, for most quarterbacks a kicking situation. For me a flick of the switch to another channel, and life or death in the soapy window. The machine is stuck—with an over-flow, and no change for another load. What to do? I got up in a flash and found another way through to the closet where my winter outfit dangles. I had a date with my baby, I speculated. The sadness of my baby is ill-conceived, as is all primary emotion in our time. That suddenly caught me lonesome and I exited to the court-yard of our sanitarium where I loved to behold the birds when it wasn't raining. This time, the rain. I hid under the eaves by the window of Nelly Bloomgarden, the typhoid carrier, and was stopped dead in my tracks. She'd been in that room since 1897. I could see her through the barred window lying on her side and watching the TV a generous party had donated. She didn't like football. It was a first down with the ball on the thirty. How had they done it? The windup. The pitch. From behind a tree she tosses a mudball at me. "That's no way to do your hunting," I call, whoever she is. She's no temptress. I remember what he asked me now. He said, "What's the score?" That's a peculiar question to ask when the answer I gave was what I said at the outset. "The score?" The score is that nothing is happening in my heart, not even the action so familiar, you know, and one has to exercise those muscles to keep their tone. For a while I relax on the bus back, but when she has to get off she finds that I have closed my fist around the seat bar over her long and smelly hair. "Ouch. I missed my stop." She was sitting in front of me, unarmed, unfortunately, because I'd make a nice roast for her table. Why do they all make out she's a woman, anyway? Couldn't she be the great Jim Brown when she says to me, "Let's run off and get married just on the spur of the moment?" How do you answer a question like that without dropping her hair which my habit is to put in my mouth? We sprint off together like in the Musical Comedies and head right for a supermarket where we buy the aforementioned roast and by the time we're back at the place it's a marriage feast and we nibble on that. "Turn off the damn box," she says. "Are you a temptress or a huntress?" I ask. The ball has changed hands and those were on the offense who now are on the defense. It's time to go out and get blazing drunk, so I step to the threshold on my way and Blooey—I'm had in the arm in the back of the neck in the right loin. Next time you won't catch me marrying a you-know-what. The air is sharp and clear, the winds are crisp, the ground crunchy underfoot, a perfect day for the game. First, I hustle down to the market by the docks where beggars scoop fishscraps and I look around for a poor girl there because I want to fuck. Better to fuck a poor girl from the docks than a rich one who can afford weaponry. I dig one up covered with muck, the scales of carp stuck in the dirt on her wrist and forearms, and I buy her from her father for a song.

> *I'm sizing up your daughter*
> *Who lives here by the water*
> *I might save her from the slaughter*
> *When the other fishes caught her.*

And she delights me with some verses of her own:

> *One evening yet to come you will limp to the high roof*
> *garden*
> *And bubbles from the lip of a peach will bust on your*
> *sniffer.*

Ah, the twentieth century hustles by like a centipede, how I love it, how we all behave in it as if it were the twenty-first. Yes, it's exhilarating, it's a bulge in the flow of events. All I need to do is turn my back and anything will happen. It's happening now, but when I reverse my field it will be too late. What happened? Well, I scrubbed her with a hemp rag and she came out pretty and bright as a nickel. When the medical student who lived below us fell in love with her glands I released her to marry him. "Be the huntress, not the temptress," I advised her; or was it, "Be the temptress, not the huntress?" Anyway half time was just over and I can't bear to hear a kick-off so I turn down the sound and leave the glimmer. The air above the atmosphere of the city is full of jets going South for the winter. South. What a stupendous idea. I buy a rucksack, Bicycle playing cards, a sackful of lotions, and an automatic needle-threader, and head South myself, or rather with a free-living beauty I meet on the bum. We got to the beach and dropped into the water and lay around like cantaloupes getting tan. The girl was a bronze athletic type that you find sometimes on the beach and sometimes you don't. She met a Persian gymnast there and we all made love on a trampoline till I was out of the question. I looked at my watch and saw it ticking. "You're not a temptress," I said. "I'm a hunter," she said. I got out of there quick as a wink, arrows wobbling by, and to mine own self I was true. The game was finished, the final score 26–17, though I don't know who won, but those of you who know me realize it all adds up to forty-three, and so you've got it.

IN OUR THYME

for Richard Tum Suden

CHAPTER 22
CHAPTER 20 CHAPTER 8
~~CHAPTER~~ sp unreal.
This is the work of
genius and free speech.
It's done with ~~stupidity~~ scooter under a
needle ~~...~~ feet she
If society ~~...~~ have
where wou ~~...~~ of a
I to ~~...~~ fabulous
Contest ~~...~~ me
once ~~...~~ ore
now ~~...~~ ance
held ~~...~~ you
~~...~~ ness
wa ~~...~~ 's
in the ~~...~~ sel
sting ~~...~~ ous
~~...~~ sism.
~~...~~ sweet
~~...~~ remem-
bring ~~...~~ love
~~...~~ you
~~...~~ ver
~~...~~ past
poems ~~...~~ san
public ~~...~~ llant.
~~...~~ ce I'm
insult ~~...~~ lay
never ~~...~~ d-
myself ~~...~~ passion
called ~~...~~ ot
snaps ~~...~~ rk,
his c ~~...~~ rested.
Lakes ~~...~~ Some kiss
~~...~~ ion.
flip ~~...~~ the
~~...~~ and
Respectability ~~...~~ crutches.
madness. ~~...~~ cracky.
Beef. I said that because you can't
communicate with such a frill.
He's a pump-attendant without a
hose. I've got some aches, and he
follows suit, so that's our com-
panionhood.

CHAPTER 8

Bless the little souls of feet she
walks on. Could you ever have
believed that such a knuckle of a
girl would turn up at the fabulous
Martha?

May the sponge of righteousness
pummel the flanks of truth.

--When to the sessions of sweet
silent clap/I summon up remem-
brance of chomp.

--What are you? Some kind of
in-group?

Oh blues, I got blues, and I'm
feeling so damp.

"Sentimentality is the heart
fornicating in a vacuum tube
with the plural of spoons."

(continued on page 43) 45

MYTHOLOGY: PLASTIC MAN

for Harry Rogan

Some people have all the money, some have all the luck, and some have all the brains, and those who have all three have luck, money and brains. I can't say it matters to me now because I'm too old, but for some people every door opens on wealth, fame or power and every road bends toward success. It's a good thing there is a different type of person too because I'm one of them, and that's a comfort. I can't say that I've had nothing, because I've had a bit; that is, I've lived this long and I've rarely been hungry, though I've been scared. The best thing to do is to keep moving, which I do, because then I don't have to pay rent, not that I mind paying rent if I like the place I'm at. I just don't like to pay it to Plastic Man, but that's the other end of the story, and we'll cross over to it when we've picked around a while on this end. I'm a prospector, you see, and that keeps me moving. I look for just about anything and sometimes I have a little bit of luck. That's not always so lucky, as you'll find out, as I found out too late in the game.

At first it was just my "love of the great outdoors" and who cared if I found nothing or not? I was young. I could look time in the face and tell him to brush his teeth. I'd do it on foot, or take a horse and a couple of mules, stuff the pack-saddles and go. I could stay as long as I had grub, and then some. That living went on for a while at a great rate, but whatever a guy is doing, there always comes a time when he figures if he's putting so much in he ought to be getting something out. That was when I first began to see the sign on the desert. I was crossing this wide, arid valley, nothing growing but sage and tumbleweed, bronco grass, crested wheat, chaparral, rabbit brush, mahoganies on the mountains, willows in the canyons and chokecherry by the springs. Suddenly a whole mountain sat in front of me that looked heavy with minerals, sparkly outcroppings on it, and a slide the color of doeskin. The sight of it yanked at my feet and told them to step up. Then I saw the old sign nailed to a wooden stake. It was quite faded, and looked insignificant, so I didn't pay any attention to it though I noticed it said: ALL THIS BELONGS TO PLASTIC MAN. I thought that was amusing, probably put there by someone with a sense of humor, who read comic books. I pushed on into the hills and stooped at a spring to fill my water bags and water my horse and my mule. When I cleared the gravel off an old piece of tin that lay there in the spring I noticed there was some printing on it, almost rusted out. ALL THIS BELONGS TO PLASTIC MAN, it said. The thought "perhaps this is a remnant of the ridiculous lost city of Ult" crossed my mind, while the thought "This isn't a Shoshone landmark" crossed it from the other direction, leaving me without a thought. Nobody owned that country, because nobody could need to own it, it was so barren and so big. Hardly a road crossed it. Well, I crossed the ridge and prospected for a few days and was surprised to find, though I ranged pretty wide, that same sign poking up here and there. I just went on with my prospecting. What I finally found was some outcroppings veined with high-grade cinnabar. I picked out some samples, staked three claims, and figured on heading for the assayer's and the land office in a couple of days. I'd take the samples and my map, get over the red tape, and come back as fast as I could. The morning I was to leave I took an early walk around my claims and noticed a fresh sign tacked up on each of the stakes. ALL THIS BELONGS TO PLASTIC MAN. Someone had come in the night, without my knowing it and had slapped up the signs. From where did they come? What did they mean by PLASTIC MAN? I decided to solve that mystery when I got back.

"Did you ever hear about Plastic Man?" I asked at the land office. They looked at me as if I'd eaten locoweed. "Did you ever see the signs he put up all over the desert out there?"

"Never been out there," said the land office man, and he looked for something in his drawer.

I registered the claims and took a couple of days to get rigged with powder, hand steels, fuse and grub and then I started back. I didn't expect I'd be leaving till the first signs of snow. It felt good when I saw again where I was going, like a home, except there was something peculiar about it, a kind of dull glitter from the distance, like a film of mucous over my claims. About a mile away my horse got jumpy and so did I, but not the mules, so we kept going. It seemed impossible. All three of my claims, from edge to edge, every rock, every bit of sagebrush was covered with a film of clear plastic so slick and hard even the mules couldn't get a footing on it. The big sign in the middle said, ALL THIS BELONGS TO PLASTIC MAN. Well, I thought, let's see. I figured I'd drill a hole to blast the plastic out of there,

49

but my hand steel wouldn't even scratch the surface. I put five sticks of powder on the surface with a two-minute fuse and took shelter down the hill. I still don't know what happened to the grub, my horse, the rest of my outfit, or to the plastic. I never woke up till I don't know when and after I did I wasn't anywhere I knew about. It was brand new, whatever it was, and it smelled like a room, and was slick and slippery wherever you touched it, and I was inside. Pretty soon a piece of it pulled open like a door and a man in a gummy suit told me that I had to get ready to meet Plastic Man. He was in a bigger one of those chambers with softer walls and everything there had the special glitter my claims had before I lost them. Plastic Man was bent over like a U bolt stuck in the ground. "Why is he bent over like that?" I asked a man in a gummy suit. "Plastic Man can't straighten up," he said. I sized up that situation and then asked for an iron, a heating pad, or anything hot. While he went to get it I rolled up my sleeves. Plastic Man didn't seem to be in pain. He winked at me between his legs like the son of a bitch that he was. "You see what happens when you're made of plastic," he said. They brought me a kind of heated rolling pin, and I began immediately to roll it over his back. Pretty soon he straightened out just like a bean sprout, and he wrapped each of his arms around me three times as if he couldn't have straightened out himself if he had wanted to. He apologized for what he had done to my claims but told me I should have read the signs. I told him I did read the signs, but that I didn't believe in Plastic Man, so I paid them no mind. He laughed at that and asked if I believed in Plastic Man now. I laughed at that. We chatted for a while over fancy sardine sandwiches and lemonade and then he could see I was getting ready to mosey on. "Here you are, have a glittering trinket for your glove compartment," he said, handing me a glittering trinket. "There is no glove compartment on my mule," I answered. "Well, keep it for an hour, then give it to your kids." He shook my hand.

"Why don't you," he said, just before I moseyed along, "go in with me fifty-fifty on developing that property. Fifty-fifty."

"Thanks, Stretch," I said. "But no thanks." And maybe that was my big mistake, but I didn't want to have anything, nothing, to do with Plastic Man. "I'll just be on my way. I'll mosey along." Now, he didn't try to stop me from moseying, but since then things have never been the same. I keep moving, but everywhere I go, far or wide, there's a sign that says, ALL THIS BELONGS TO PLASTIC MAN. Every little prospect I try to develop never works out any more. He doesn't cover my claims with plastic like he used to, but this is what happens. Usually when I'm ready to put in my first round I suddenly feel his long arm wrap around me—gently—and I'm back having some fancy sandwiches and a Pepsi and the same conversation with Plastic Man. I don't know if he'll ever give up, but it's nothing doing for me. I'm not one of those. So I keep moving because I don't want to pay the rent to Plastic Man, and though it can't possibly ever come out right, I hope to edge out of it some day.

MYTHOLOGY: HERMES

The Head Librarian said he was a whiz. Hermes was the swiftest page in the stacks, who could remove a book for you almost before the request was in. And could he ever read. He finished a volume quicker than most people learned how to swim. Back in the old days they used to call him Hermes because he was like quicksilver, and one of the reasons was that he didn't eat. He didn't eat so much his girl friend got fat worrying about the leftovers, and it got so that Hermes could circle her forty-three times walking from his house to hers, whereas in the old days he could circle her only forty-three times, too, seeing how she got wider but also walked slower. Most living creatures on the face of the earth were no match for Hermes. They dropped dead of exhaustion, including the fabled Winnemucca centipede. Some people knew that he could outrun Swift Old Death, because Hermes was so old, but so was his girl friend, and she couldn't run at all. Some day maybe all the best stories of

Hermes can be told, but you can't keep up with them they happen so fast. There is at least one that most deserves the telling, a story the Head Librarian likes to recount, and that story is the one we'll tell, as soon as we get around to it. Hermes' girl friend was as slow as he was fast, and that was why she couldn't get him fed, but it wasn't her fault, because the only chance the girl had was when he fell asleep and he could get a good night's sleep in the blink of an eye, while the girl friend had hardly begun to stir the pudding, and she liked to lick the spoon. For all everybody knew Hermes could have eaten just the same, quicker than anyone else could see. The grub in and out so quick it never had a chance to change color; he just skimmed off the nutrition and left the rest on the table. That probably explains why everyone got slower while Hermes is always quicker. He can steal something, use it up, and return it in better-than-new condition between the time the owner decides to use it and goes to the closet to get it. He once stole a whole church picnic, hustled it over to feed a batch of Orientals, and got it back clean and empty so quick the church elders believed they must have already eaten it themselves. They rubbed their stomachs, packed up, and went home to watch the war on color TV.

The best story is still the one the Head Librarian tells, which we are coming to eventually. It was because of him, you remember, that automation never came to our library. That was the time they got up for us one of the slickest, quickest, prettiest IBM automatic book retrievers that ever read a book spine. It had blinking lights and buttons and I don't know what all, and it made the noise of a sweetheart. Hermes didn't care one bit. He just warmed up by running from here to Bogalusa, to Winnipeg, and back here, while most of us were eating breakfast. They brought down from the university one of the smartest men you ever wanted to see, one of those young, fresh ones with soft hair on his cheeks and two pair of glasses. You could see that there were the names of more books in his head than people who swim for pleasure. Everybody turned out, and they threw up a huge grandstand, and they sold lime juice in plastic cups. It was something. The professor with that bland academic sneer on his face looked at Hermes, who wasn't much to see, and signaled he was ready to begin. They plugged in their IBM beauty till it puckered up and started to blink like an army division looking for its contact lenses in an olympic-sized chlorinated pool. The pretty lady, whom we'll call the operator, signaled GO. It wasn't even a contest. Hermes took one look at the professor coming to the counter, disappeared, and reappeared almost immediately with seven books, just as the professor handed the request card to the operator (who wasn't a bad twist herself). Six of the books were those six written on the card, but when the professor saw the seventh his face turned yellow and then bright orange, his tongue went dry, and his eyeballs whirled in their sockets.

"This is absolutely remarkable, commendable, and straight-A work," he snorted. "This book is one I've had an interlibrary urgent search-and-find slip on for two years now." He reached over to shake Hermes' hand but grabbed only a slim puff of wind. Hermes' girl was bobbing up and down in a wobbly celebration. Everyone cheered, but no one was surprised, because everyone knew that Hermes could outrun even Swift Old Death, running him so fast through our town that he'd have to quit, and sit down on the outskirts, panting, and more often than no pass the people by. But the best story is the one the Head Librarian tells, which we'll come to presently, if not now, one which she tells to children from the porch of the huge old building that used to be the library, which faces our brand new blinker and hummer called The Information Central, that no one ever enters. It's the story of the great library fire, and how it happened, though no one knows how it began, but things have never been the same. It was Hermes, who is as quick with his nose as he is with his feet, who first smelled the smoke, and he speeded through the stacks to find the fire extinguishers, but the one on the first floor was empty, and on the second, and the third the same. The flames followed Hermes like a blaze through dry brush. On the seventh floor he found the only full one and spun around with the foam spewing to hit the Head Librarian flush. Well, I guess this story isn't so good, the usual silly slapstick from here on, and it's not worth telling again, and it has been so long since I rose up and told a story that I forgot. Goodby.

CHAPTER 3

Oh honey, it is a crummy
bit of treatment, but nothing
spreads without heat and the
smell of a horse.

 (continued on page 43)

MYTHOLOGY: WONDER WOMAN

Wonder Woman was a dike, but she was nice. If she hadn't been a dike she might have been nice, but she wouldn't have been Wonder Woman, and vice-versa. Of all the interesting stories about Wonder Woman, the most delightful is the tale of how she ended the war in Vietnam. When she started to end it it wasn't over but when she was through it was finished. Except nobody believed a dike could end the war. They went on killing like the bunch of rowdies they believed in. Finally everybody was crowded into the bloodshed till there was no one left on earth except Wonder Woman and one slow-moving little squirt with asthma. She met him on the road, where you meet everyone these days in case of emergency. He was trying to push his car uphill at a total stalemate when Wonder Woman surprised him.

"What's the big idea, buster," she intoned.

The car slid backwards into a warehouse of surplus feathers. "I'm not very anxious," he said.

"You're the last man here on earth so you should be bawling your ass off."

"You too should be weeping, for you are the last woman on earth as far as is imaginable." He leaned on the shoulder of the freeway.

"If you want to have the straight goop, I'm Wonder Woman, the dike." She blew on her wristlets. "But why do you insist on pushing around that old jalopy, when here for the asking are all these Cadillacs and Chaparrals?"

"My analyst is dead," he roared.

"Just hop in and drive one of them away, and don't bother me."

"There's no place I want to go. It's death, death, everywhere death. All the people are dead as doornails. I never thought I'd live to see the day."

"At least the traffic is light. Haw Haw." Wonder Woman fixed her comb and prepared to leave.

"I guess I could drive East through Canada. I always wanted to drive East through Canada, and why not? It's a beautiful country and a friendly place. Thank you for the wonderful idea, Wonder Woman." He reached a long arm out and dragged himself over to a solid blue Mercedes 300 and tipped out the ex-driver. The motor gurgled when he hit the switch.

Wonder Woman split for elsewhere. She visited the hangouts of her old consorts: Cynthia the Sphincter was dead, as were Julie and Fatty and Leslie the Mars Bar. She went to Pittsburgh. She headed for Santa Cruz. She got to Albany. She hit Moose Jaw. She stopped in Philly. She took in New York City. She crossed to Budapest. Copenhagen was empty. Damascus was empty. Kuala Lumpur was through. The little wheezer had been right. She journeyed to New Delhi. She hit Kyoto in the spring. She left for Singapore. She hustled to Djakarta. They all were dead. Everyone was dead. She decided to take in a movie. Best of all was a revival of the old blue whisker comedies, which she took in with a cup of buttered popcorn that tasted disturbingly fresh. Without her cohorts she fell into a fit of depression. Then she saw an airplane overhead and shot it down in her excitement. Luckily there was nobody aboard except for one newspaper. The flyer read TALK BUYS MUD FLAP and the headlines, REVERSE PUMP MURTY. The mention of Pump Murty kept Wonder Woman's chin up. "So," she thought. "Even at the end the old guy could wrap a rice patch."* Then she fell into a fit of depression. All around her heavy machinery was hanging out as if it had a contract to work. "For naught. For naught. For naught," she sighed and then hopped onto a Caterpillar DB and started pushing everything aside until she uncovered the remains of a familiar solid blue Mercedes. She rolled it over and over down a side street. Poor little guy. "Fuck ambition," she screamed, standing up and waving her arms around. Suddenly the bulldozer veered out of control into a huge man-made wall which toppled on top of her knocking her for a loop, and squooshing her down in a pit of depression. When she came to she wasn't herself but was being cared for by a slowpoke with asthma. "There now," he said. "You had quite a seizure."

"Where am I?" Wonder Woman queried. "And what kind of special clothing is this?"

"You are Wonder Woman, the last dike on earth," said the slow one. "Admired and esteemed by the whole world, which is me."

"Chubby chance of that, you handsome stud, you fistful of nuts," and she threw her weakened arms around his neck. He mopped her lecherous brow with droplets

* special dike talk or professional dyke jargon.

from a nearby rivulet. She began to sigh and swivel. He worked on her clothes with a hacksaw till they fell apart like a shutter. He was staring at the last cunt on earth. He untied from his leg the last cock on earth and when she saw it she sizzled. "Do something filthy dirty right away."

"But you're Wonder Woman, the dike," he slobbered, holding his cock at arm's length. Just then she passed a sonorous and intoxicating flatus that drugged them into an ecstatic embrace, pumping and sucking like it was the end of the world. He wondered if she was still Wonder Woman if she wasn't a dike, but was so nice. She cooked his dinner and mended his sock and then they started to have babies, and the babies they had were made of gold.

CHAPTER 10

He held us spellbound in his
variety of thoughts. I could
have even touched him a little despite the flakes, but oh
the horror of an upbringing
built on caution as its pinnacle.

Everyone is stingier, though
life today is effortless and
glideproof, except, of course,
the fortunate festival temptress
who was the talk of '43.

Oh honey, it is a crummy
bit of treatment, but nothing
spreads without heat and the
smell of a horse.

 (*continued on page 43*)

KELLY

It all starts with a murder, he knocks off a woman, somebody's wife, the killing backs up the blood in the veins; but
then I always get lost because I can't stop saying whatever
there is to say about Kelly, no matter what else I have to do,
because it's not such a cinch to believe in a man who has
done nothing in his life but change position, and that not
frequently, though I'll admit he has followed me around like
the tail of a kite, because wherever I did what I did, no matter
right or wrong, Kelly showed up in the midst, and that's not
simple because I move around the globe a lot, being a world
traveler. So I always end up telling the story I'm not telling,
which is different from what I've begun to tell. Wherever I go,
whatever I say, Kelly's there with something living on him.
"Hello, Kelly," but he never makes a remark. He's just there,
not to help, but he's there, punctuating my eyesight. It might
be irrelevant, but he's the only Jewish Kelly I've ever known.
Don't get me wrong, I'm Jewish too, but the Jewishness of
Kelly astounds and mystifies. There'll be no more said on the

subject, because even though a Jew, he's best at doing noth-ing. Nothing. He's a man with absolutely nothing on the ball, and that's what I admire in him. Only once in the whole time I've spotted him spotting me has he ever come close to mut-tering a word, and that not even a real word; even though sometimes I usually run around with a daughter of his. He just looks at me as if he's looking the other way, but it never fails that if the time is ripe he turns up, bland. I can tell you a story so incredible to believe that I'm ashamed to tell it; in fact, I'm ashamed to tell every story that's about me, because I've had quite a humdinger of a life. I've hitchhiked my ass off on every continent, back and forth, and it's ridiculous because there's not supposed to be a Jewish hitchhiker in the picture. Listen, then, as I unweave my plaintive saga. Sinbad, I'm not; but I've had a trip or two.

The first installment comes on a bus from Kashmir to Delhi where we were going back to our ship (about which some more later) so we could leave the subcontinent and head out into the Sea of Japan, just for kicks. Kashmir was a beauty place with lakes and mountains and little people and other such exotic splendor. Instead of the new bus we were prom-ised at the tourist office we got an old honker and wheezer, but with only four people aboard we weren't too uncomfort-able. But what happened? It was supposed to be a fifteen-hour ride and that was what I called "fat chance." About eleven hours into the ride we meet brother bus that is supposed to be heading for Kashmir, but it's up on jacks by the side of the road and ten men are underneath it. Our driver pulls over, gives us some instructions in his own dialect, and goes into conference with the opposite driver. I observe that we have learned some patience in the East and she presses my thigh with the ball of her palm. Whenever I say something right she touches me. If something happens to her I will leave the world. Suddenly all the passengers from brother bus, which was filled to the brim, start filing over to our bus, Kelly, of course, among them. I couldn't believe what was going on. They were coming to take over our bus to go the other way. "What is this joke?" I ask her. She is weeping. "They're going to make us switch buses." "We'll stick it out," I assure her. "Defend your seat." And we set ourselves, recalling the long sit-ins of our youth. Kelly is watching us. "Kelly," I say. "Is this what happens in real life?" Of course Kelly doesn't even spare us a grimace. He has a bundle under his arm that is wriggling and it's an effort to keep it still. Naturally we have to shift into the broken bus and there we sit, ad infinitum. "Who is that Kelly, anyway," she asks while we wait. "Some good-for-nothing," I say. "Some good-for-nothing who always shows up." We get to Delhi one and a half days later, so tired we just stay in the cabin of my boat, snoozing and fucking. Fucking her is like halving the sun.

Now I'll tell you about the time I was hitching down through Egypt and Nigeria back to the Sudan and on into Ghana, on my way to South Africa because I wanted to make some of their money. We were at the Liberian frontier, trying to pass into Zambia, and we got out of Liberia O.K. but Zambia customs got tough. "How much money you got?" they asked. "Twenty-two dollars," I replied. "How much money you got?" they asked my friend. "Nothing," she said, showing her empty pretty palms. "You each need to have fifty dollars." "That means one hundred dollars?" "Yes." "Look, we're just passing through your little country to South Africa and it's such a narrow country; half a day and we'll be gone. What good is a hundred dollars?" "It will get you through Zambia. Otherwise, no." That was it. We tripped gaily back to the Liberian officials and faced them with our problem. "Do you expect," they said politely, "that we will let you back in our country when you have been rejected by those others?" There was no facing that logic. We were stuck. Here was a little thirty-meter strip between two flags, and she said to me, "It's not much, but we'll have to call it home. I'll knit us a flag of our own." It was a sour laugh we had over that joke. Nowhere. Nothing. Not a rock to sit on, not a coffee house, not a vegetable growing. All we could do was toss our bedrolls on the ground and lean on them. It shook me up when she unexpectedly began to cry. She was no weakling but she was a woman, and sometimes they cry. "What will we do?" she asked. "We'll sit here for a while," I said. It was ugly there, between two countries, but we didn't move for at least three hours, sighing, burping and wheezing and once in a while I slurped on her lips to hush her complaints. Just at that time, an hour or so before sundown, a time when you know the day isn't endless and you've got to move or else it will be dark, a man walks out of the Liberian exit heading for the Zambian entrance. He's turned out pretty well because only up close can you see that his tweed is threadbare. He pauses a moment to look at us in our misery. It's Kelly. "Kelly," I say. "Kelly, here we are. Look where we have to snuggle up." I can see something thumping from inside his duffel. He doesn't even change expression, but shoves on, and slips through Zambian customs as if he were born there. That's when I spring into action. "Look," I tell the measly little official behind the desk, who looks at my white skin as if it were the pox. "Look. You've got to let us in. There's not a question in my mind. We can't stay on that nowhere piece of dirt forever." "One hundred dollars, even say fifty between you. Show me fifty dollars. Regulations can . . ." I grab him by the lapels and begin to rattle the pens in his pocket. Two huge border guards rip me off his desk and drag me back to no man's land where she's watching. If they touch her I vow I'd destroy the world. They don't, but they work me over till I'm bloody. I just lie there still as a bone for a moment because what they did to me was painful, though I've been hurt more in my life.

"Get up and come with us." At any border but this that would have sounded scary, but not here. It was the Liberian border police. They took pity on us when they saw me beat up, and gave us an empty corner of their country to spend the night in, and in the morning sent us on our way overland through a swamp to the Somali border only fifteen kilometers away. It was no easy slog through the swamp where who knows what kind of snakes and leeches kept eyeing us. Once an alligator walked right up to us and bared his teeth. "Be gone," I said. "We've got enough troubles without you." We were up to our hips in muck, and my friend has such special tender hips. At the Somali border there was a friendly reception for us; even Kelly was there, but how he got there is a story he'll have to tell.

Even though I never took much time to learn anything in my life I did find out how to sail, and in fact at one time I held valid captain's papers, which is no picayune accomplishment, I must be proud to say. Traveling with her in my own boat is sometimes beautiful because the sea is placid, but if the sea is rugged you could wish you were walking. Some day I'll demonstrate the scars. We were sailing here and there on the Mediterranean, which in my opinion is a top-notch sea, and we slipped into a little port called Macaroon, on the Eastern end of the Libyan coast. We waited there for a good three hours till the customs officials came aboard, and by that time the baby was crying, and that rattled us a bit, because the kid wasn't ours and we were hiding it under a mop. That, however, wasn't what bothered the customs officials. You see, we had sailed from the little dock at Beersheba a few weeks before after some splendid sailfishing in the Dead Sea, and Israel was our last real port of call. They hadn't stamped our passports but I had got a vaccination there and had the Israeli Yellow Fever Stamp on my health certificate. One look at that and they nabbed me. "You're a spy for the enemy." "What enemy?" "Our enemy." "Oh, shit. That's just untrue. I'm not a spy, I'm a sailor." By then they had shoved me around a little, and had handcuffed my wrists to my ankles. They grabbed the woman of my ship by her spicy arms. They'd better be careful what they're doing, I was thinking, because I have power they couldn't dream about. "We're going to kill your husband," they told her. She shrugged. Maybe she thought they were speaking Arabic. Well, they rolled me off to their police station for two days and kept me awake so they could pick on me and ask stupid questions, and believe me I wish I had some answers because I would have squealed. They were causing me pain, with my pinky in a vice, and that queer sadist threatening my gotchkis with a blade. After a couple of days of heartache, they let me go, and who knows why. They could have killed me and no one would have been the worse for it. As I was leaving through the front door you know already who I saw standing at the sergeant's desk as if he were a special agent. Kelly. "Kelly," I said. "What have you been up to around here?" He wouldn't even look at me, but stood there fingering something that was alive in his hand. At that point I must say my relationship with Kelly was at an all-time low. What was he? I thought. He was just there. He wasn't even a good smoky cup of tea. Who needs, I thought at that time, such a Kelly as this? I almost told the Arabs that he was the Jewish spy, but fuck it, I thought; I was happy enough to get back to my woman, my ship, and to sail away into a snappy Mediterranean sunset.

For the next installment I am trying to get out of a Caribbean port that shall go unmentioned for political reasons and I notice I'm locked in the harbor by a large ship that looks like a junk, or one of those half-moon tubs you see tooling up the Bosporus, but much bigger, sitting high in the water with its holds empty. I decide it's best to go ashore and find the owner to tell him I plan to weigh anchor in just a couple of hours. He was easy to find, sitting in the first café where I inquired. He wasn't an ordinary-looking man, nor was he strange; in fact, he didn't even look interesting, so we made friends immediately and he insisted that before he move the ship I should come spend a few hours aboard. I agreed and suggested that we set right out so I wouldn't lose much time, but he thought it best if he set out first to give himself time to tie up his monkey.

"I don't mind a monkey," I say. "What the hell, a monkey."

We set out together, and clamber up the high side of his ship and I suddenly understand what he means by a monkey. It was a bull gorilla, and not a miniature, and he had painted its pus green.

"I got it in Kashmir," he said.

"How in hell did a gorilla come to Kashmir?" I asked.

"That's why I got it. They wanted to get rid of it." The beast was shackled to a bulkhead with a long chain and was looking at me, chuckling to himself. He finally made a lunge for my ankle as soon as he thought I was close enough. If I didn't have the reflexes of a bear he would have got a grip on me. We stood there staring at each other for a long time until words came to my mouth out of the blue.

"Kelly," I said. "Kelly. Kelly. What a pity and a shame. What trick of fate has made you turn out so?"

Kelly stared into my human eyes for a long moment, and then shrugged. That shrug, believe me, was the closest Kelly ever came to saying a word to me.

My host pacified the brute and then gave me a tour of the ship. It was filthy, refuse heaped all over the decks and practically filling the two cabins—busted trunks, rusty C-rations, heaps of Cutty Sark empties, rotting tamarinds. He offered to take me down to the hold, which I wasn't very anxious to see, judging by the state of things above. Just the same I followed him and was surprised to find the hold full of neatly arranged wooden crates.

"Those crates must be empty," I said. "You're riding so high in the water."

"Quite to the contrary," he said, and he opened one. The crate was full of old but polished machine parts each carefully numbered and placed like stones at an excavation. He indicated that all the other crates were similarly full. It was a mystery to me how he rode so high because with the cargo he carried the water line should have been at the gunwale. I started to ask some questions to see if I could find out more about it.

"Where are you headed sir, with this cargo aboard?" I inquired as a start.

"I'm looking for the man who murdered my wife," he hollered.

CHAPTER 2

Contentment. The pull that
once was possible is empty
now, though I offer you
this with threadbare lungs.
Are you a dove or a security risk?

The door opened on a room
packed with furry infants, all
of whom were born reciting
poems, though the general
public has been kept out in the
dark.

(continued on page 43)

5 MYTHOLOGIES

CHAPTER 24

I wooda hittim, what he said
about art, about egoplasti-
forminousautohostilaphonic
art. I cooda ticked him in
the lobes, snooched his puss.

It is widely believed that a man
can be told by his blundering
noise, but put no truck, because
upstairs it counts.

Timeless emotion
is the result of hours
of cataloging.

Certain bits of fruit are just in-
fatuating: the prune, the exotic
citron, the impossible watermelon. These fruits have a quiet.
energetic presence, like an ex-
plosive discotheque location.
Otherwise it's a slump you're in.

(continued on page 43) 79

MYTHOLOGY: THOMAS

A man there was called Thomas who in the aged long ago time before I was a boy was the man of many creatures, a many-creatured man in the hills before my youth of which one, and there was only one in the park across the street where there were no apple trees, no bushelfuls of apples to tumble to our baskets, though we held them up into the hushed evenings of hope when we were hopeless in the spring of asphalt freshets, and the earth abounded beneath it, we thought, and sang all hours of artichokes and pomegranates, quinces and loquats, though we had none, nor could we sing where the sun in the air like smoked crystal coughed, and the rivulets rippled through our Springmaid, chamber-tossed apartment and lapped against our father at his pinochle in the kitchen, who never saw him, who never would, our Thomas, where he stood in the windfall autumn light presaging school, which we dreaded as the vulture dreads the fountain of youth, when youth will go on forever until it becomes commonplace across the street to see kids, who can understand but will never care for the golden arguments of Thomas with his tedious assignment, for the tedium of youth is long enough to misconstrue when God is around, within, above, about, beneath and before us, in every marble, in every penny we illegally pitch, and he's under the steps, and in the bottle of Absorbine Jr. and has forsaken his flock to come play with our championship sleepers and we called him, "Thomas," and he said, "Hold your breath for a minute." He turned up his Zenith to catch the score.

"Three up," he said. "Bottom of the sixth."

Maybe we had Thomas all wrong. Every week, after we got our allowances, we'd sit around with him playing draw poker and he'd tell us how he killed a man once and served fourteen years of it, and how he'd do it again if he had fourteen more years. He had more than that, though we weren't smart enough to tell him. We were delighted because he was the only guy we knew who had ever murdered another guy, and we begged him to do it again, but he was embarrassed. "Shut up, you shrimps," he'd say and pretend to listen to the ball game while he skinned us, but we didn't mind, because we were youths, and then we grew up, and then he said he'd kill us, so we made out we were kids again and played poker with him against our better judgment. This time Billy won and Thomas pulled a knife, but Billy had a zip gun and he killed Thomas, and that's how Billy got his transistor radio which doesn't work anymore.

Well, to shorten this long story about Thomas let me sum up: Ray quit school first and joined the Marines; Billy disappeared and nobody ever heard from him again; Tony went to college and became a science teacher; Andy has got himself a line of girls and is socking it away; Tish got a job as a runner on Wall Street and became a broker;

John Blue works in a machine shop; Phil is a junkie; Jack Schneider drives a cab; Albert played Double-A ball for a while but was too small and now works as a coach; Rico became a pharmacist and still lives with his mother; Quinlan got a job down on Madison Avenue, but he's a faggot; Bert writes books; Rasey and Deuce run a filling station; Hubby has got a bunch of kids and works downtown at two jobs; nobody knows what happened to Plooky; Rosemarie was always one of the boys, and still is; Flynn went out West but now he's back and hangs out at the same bar his dad did; Milt owns a hardware store; Archie works in an office and fishes on weekends; Nick is happy as a dentist; Roger, Dan, Solly, Schultz and Norris all went nuts; you still see Powers around, but nobody knows what he does. I guess that's all, except for my gang, but this story is about Thomas.

A few weeks later Thomas shows up just when everybody thinks he's dead, and this time he's got a great big fur coat to wear with his beard and long hair. A few years later he asks me a question. "What happened to that kid Billy? He's got my radio." I tell him that I don't know, because Billy just disappeared and was never heard from again. Just then Billy shows up and Thomas pulls a knife and threatens to kill him if he doesn't give back the radio. "It's my radio in the first place," he says. But Billy's got a billy club and he beats Thomas across the side of his head and when he's down he takes the knife away and sticks him and then pushes his face in just for kicks so he's dead and then Billy disappears and is never heard from again. We all chip in to buy Thomas a good funeral with a big box, because he's the biggest man we know, and wanted to be buried with his coat on because he never really wore it enough.

When the war came everybody and his buddy

enlisted because we figured it was up to us to preserve our way of life so our kids would have it in the years to come, except Hubby didn't go because he had too many kids, so he went to work in a munitions factory that blew up and he died. Most of the gang died in the war including me, but first I have to finish this story.

On the next week after the war Thomas came back and everyone cried to see him because how come they died and he could come back afterwards? The neighborhood hadn't changed much except the Porto Ricans were moving in and out so fast it scared the Germans. Everyone went to eat Chinks in Chinatown a lot and ordered the number three dinner for four. There were six of them. "I wish I knew what happened to Billy," Thomas said. "That kid who got my transistor radio that time." It couldn't have mattered much because he had a brand new shortwave transistor set he had heisted somewhere, and even one of those crystal sets we always played with when we were kids. Then Billy came back for good with the broken radio and he gave it back to Thomas and they both laughed. They have a lot in common now. They both listen to the radio a lot and you know it's them when you hear "Har, Har, Har," from Thomas. Billy says, "That kills me." They slap their knees and they slap each other's knees. Thomas has shaved and he cut his hair, but he's the same old Thomas. The old neighborhood seems just the same, otherwise. The guys stand in front of the candy store with Lennie the bookie, and Frenchy got a job as a soda jerk.

MYTHOLOGY: NASSER

There was a small unshaven man in Jerusalem called Nasser who worked at a café inside the Damascus Gate. He carried cherry-red coals to your hooka when you smoked. His clothes were a simple black smock tied with a piece of rope around the middle, a black, gold-embroidered skullcap and worn slippers. "War is ugly, but peace is lovely," he shouted when he approached to take your order. He kept your smoke bubbling through the water by bringing his coals when yours were dim. Though he always sounded angry, he wasn't, and would get you tea or coffee, or whatever else you wanted when you asked for it. He plays no more part in this saga.

Tim hiccuped and looked up at the apples. Applesauce was a delicacy he admired more than trout, and that was why he had decided not to fish long ago, though he always carried a spear gun. He went to the carnival instead, a rural affair with ostrich races, where he got twenty-five big points. He hoped somebody was making a ladder. All the sky was blue as Windex. Tim came to a shoddy stall where a small unshaven man was selling rummage. Who was this man and where did he come from and how did he get to rural America? "Get out," said Tim. "Get out and make room for a husky grownup." Tim examined the goods and found what he wanted for the apple season: a black smock, a rope belt, a black, gold-embroidered skullcap. They weren't for sale. "Get out of here," said Tim, but the man didn't budge. "It's almost apple season." When the small man persisted Tim pierced his neck with a spear and now Tim plays no more part in this saga.

"War is lovely," said General Gon to his wife, who didn't like to cook and was stingy with oranges. "Only when you are winning, and you are always winning." A man in worn slippers entered with a pan of cherry-red coals for the General's pipe. Who, why and whence? He winked at the General's wife, who followed him out the door. The General smashed his wife's stringed instrument with a treacherous war trophy.

"I asked you never to do that," the wife piped up in the doorway.

"Now you'll spend more time strumming your instrument," mumbled General Gon.

Late that night a man in a black smock tied with a rope belt entered the General's sleeping chamber with a gold-embroidered black skullcap full of napalm with which he buttered the body of General Gon, and now General Gon plays no more part in this saga.

"I don't get those hawks," said Moriarity to his three-month-old son. "They've been up to that all day. Look at the way they dive down and rip out clumps of grass and carry it way up there and then drop it on each other like kids having a dirt fight. Who's ever seen hawks at play before?"

"Jeepers, Dad," said the child. "Your eyes are sharpissimo."

From around the corner of First Avenue and Forty-sixth Street Kagowitz appeared with his child in a perambulator.

"Slow down, Dad," said the child. "There's my connection."

The Kagowitz child was small and unshaven, and he started to shout, though of course he wasn't angry. Both fathers were gazing at the fabulous New York Grasshawks. The infant tied up with a stroller strap and his connection pulled a syringe from his plastic duck and now both the Moriarity and Kagowitz families are booted out of this saga and won't play a part in any other saga until they show some self-control.

It was Harry's giddiest job and a new experience, piloting a skywriter. On the ground he had a lousy handwriting, but in the air he was the most legible of them all. That's how he landed the position, though his Peace Corps record wasn't sweet and his dossier showed too many petitions signed. Could he spell? That was the unanswered dilemma in the minds of his superiors. Harry thought he could, but didn't know what would happen in a pinch. This was it. He was desperate and traumatized, in the midst of the worst identity crisis of the season; He cruised out over the city as if it were a suburb. "War," he embroidered on the atmospheric fabric, "is homely; but peace . . ." That's all he wrote. He bailed out like a punctuation, and too bad he disappeared, because there is a lot more he could do in this saga.

"Holey Moley," said Vincent, and he threw his gold-embroidered black skullcap at the wall. "I don't get it." He was a promising young violinist.

"What's there not to get?" Noland the potential literary critic, inquired.

"This work. This saga. It's goofy." He rent his black smock to shreds and formed the rope belt into a noose.

"Give me a crack at it." Noland swaggered over to the desk.

"That's enough reading for me," said Vincent as he shoved the books into Noland's mitts. "I'm going to waste my time watching the boob tube from here on out."

Nolan read with the long hunger of a genuine book-worm until his cheeks were cherry-red. When he finally looked up there was an expression of nausea on his puss. "Why this is nothing but a . . ."

He never played a part in this saga, nor will he ever play a part in any other saga.

CHAPTER 5

Is riding a scooter under a
bridge with one leg broken
and a spent terminal what
you call gilt-edged happiness?

He had that freaky substance
on his breasts, and if you
think that wasn't memorable
you should have heard him
wink. 6 1/2 gallons of diesel
fuel before I took his name.

Love the bushy tail, but love
the antlers as well, and you
will find the roast delicious.

Is that the CAT'S PAW ROMANCE
FAMILY or the STUFFED OLIVE
CONSPIRACY?

One delves and finds the cork,
but few people are interested.
The place is fertile. Some kiss
before, some after the eruption.
Click. Click. Click.

Beef. I said that because you can't
communicate with such a frill.
He's a pump-attendant without a
hose. I've got some aches, and he
follows suit, so that's our com-
panionhood.

 (continued on page 43)

MYTHOLOGY: GOLIATH

Three men were rowing a boat on the waterway that surrounds the exposition. One was wise, one was healthy and the third was fabulously rich. The healthy one and the wise rowed the boat, while the rich one looked things over, except the wise one didn't row much. He looked around too and told of his observations, though the rich one wouldn't listen and the healthy one felt the pump that lived in his chest like an author.

"All this stuff," the rich one said, swinging his arm in a munificent arc.

"It's just the beginning," said the wise one.

Soft billowing light rose from the islands of the exposition and fell on their boat like mist. Without warning the healthy one looked up and said nothing. The boat stopped in midstream because the wise one wasn't rowing either. "What are this?" queried the wise one. "It must be a light." He responded to his own query, and then checked his compass. Then a storm blew up from thin air, tossing the boat about as if it were made of wood. The healthy one shipped his oars immediately and lay down on the bottom of the boat. The rich one lay down beside him. The wise one let his oars slip from the oarlocks and drift away. Then he lay down. All around them were the sound effects. Above them the wind howled and beside them the water-way swelled. The little boat was hoisted on the wavecrests and dropped with a resonant crack. It was early and then the three men fell asleep. The rich one dreamed he was the healthy one. The wise one dreamed the same. And the healthy one dreamed of his tongue, his liver and his lungs. When they woke up it was as if it were day, though it was night. Where had the islands of the exposition gone? They would have disappeared in the brightness of the light they had seen before the storm, though there were colors still palely visible, like a woman's flesh behind a shower cur-tain.

"There's the light again," said the wise one.

"We must go there immediately," the rich one ordered, and the healthy one began to surge at his oars like a piece of raw meat. The wise one trailed his hand in the water. "It seems warmer," he said.

"Get going. Let's get going." The rich one turned from the rower to the light, from the rower to the light. As hard as the healthy one pulled at the oars they seemed to be getting no closer to the island of light, as if a current radi-ating from the source was as swift as the motion of the boat.

"It must be," said the wise one, "that somehow the light is warming the water."

"Let me at those oars," said the rich one, and he sat down beside the healthy one, took one oar, and began trying to pull with him.

"His must be a stronger pull than yours," the wise one

conjectured, as the boat began to move in a small circle around the same point.

"If you only hadn't lost your oars," the rich one said to the wise one, and at that the oar slipped out of his hand, so it too joggled loose and floated off into another current.

"You muffin," the healthy one mumbled, lifted out his oar, stood up on the bow, and began paddling like an Indian or a gondolier. They weren't moving. The light that fell was intoxicating as a sound. Its brilliance burned out all the rest of the exposition lights, though the men themselves were left in darkness only barely able to see each other, and unable to make out the shoreline. The healthy one lifted his oar from the water, and leaned it on a seat. "It's no use," he said; just then the bow hit the beach and he was thrown overboard, recovering with an elegant backflip. They had reached the shore as if without an effort. The rich one slipped on his jacket and did up his tie, and the wise one said, "It's a mystery how we got here." One of the many strange coincidences in our story.

It seemed they were on the far end of the island from the light and though the rich one started off at a pace, the healthy one didn't want to and the wise one couldn't follow; he soon slowed down and they walked together. "We'll never get there," said the rich one.

When they were tired they camped in a gulley between two bare ridges. As if the light were a liquid it filled the gulley, casting no shadows. When they were settled the wise one told a story, to brighten up their dampened spirits. "Once there was a bird who wanted to be a fish so he fell into the water and swam and became one. Once there was a fish who wanted to be a bird so he flapped his fins and flew out of the water. Once there was a man who only wanted to be a man, but Selçuk said, 'Not yet, baby.'" The wise one looked at the other two to see how they had received his story, but it was early and they were fast asleep. Soon he was fast asleep. It was even earlier when they woke up to find they were in the middle of a crowd though none of the crowd was looking at them. The people were arranged in nearly concentric rings around the source of the light, facing away from it toward the fringes of the island. The men were closer to the source than they had imagined and they made their way toward it, touching no one in the crowd. It was neither day nor night. When they got close enough each of them expressed his surprise. "My gracious," said the healthy one. "It's huge," said the rich one. "And it looks human," said the wise one. The light was no more intense at the source than it had been anywhere else—in the boat, or on the land.

"It moves," said some nearby voices. The huge, luminous creature made a slow heavy motion with its body on the pedestal as if it were marching. The rich one looked and wondered if the clothes were made of pearl. The healthy one admired and feared the enormous muscle. And the wise one stood at the pedestal reading again and again the name carved there and painted in the colors of a nation: GOLIATH GOLIATH.

CHAPTER 20

Sometimes just one more bite and
I feel on the edge of a precipice.
Too many holidays, too many
specimens, too much stuffing.
I've got my credentials to hang me
up.

Stop vulgarity before it stops itself.
GX43tg01 is most universally admired. So are the others. Hi there,
dimples.

If you cared enough about earrings
not to be so snoopy you'd let some
decent people in with their own in-
stinctual behavior, and then you'd
note a change in the faux pas.

When it's safe and sound in bed and
snug we hope that no one will come
in through that door and ask to fuck.

"How ya doin', honey butter," was the
constant endearing phrase, but the roof
still leaked from floor to ceiling and
we weren't getting younger in our dark
pork interior.

 (continued on page 43)

MYTHOLOGY: CRANE

D was delighted with his Crane, or was he? R didn't have one, and was delightful, or was he jealous? We'll find out if we keep this up, or maybe not.

"If you keep it up," said R to D, "you'll go too far, or maybe not far enough, and by then it will be too late. But the best thing. The best thing. The best thing will be when you get rid of your Crane."

"Look out," said D. "I'm barreling through."

Through he barreled, but sans his Crane.

"The work never gets done around here," said R before he scampered out of the room like jetsam. Then he scampered back in. D spotted him and slumped back exhausted onto his Crane.

"You have your Crane," said R. "Pick yourself up." He pretended not to see the morons in the room.

"How is that done?" D interrogated.

"I can't help you if you pretend to be so cautious." R scampered out of the room again and then he ambled back in. "I see you haven't done it, or have you? So what? What good, after all, is your Crane?"

D hoisted himself up the rope near his bed and held on with one hand as he polished the ceiling mirror. "My Crane," he said, "is my . . ." he paused. "But maybe not."

"Some day you'll have to sit down carefully to explain what the Crane means. How does your life improve, day by day?"

D fell to the floor and dozed off.

"Ah hah," R sputtered. "Go ahead, sleep forever and see what good your Crane will do you then. But maybe not. When will you lack some conviction?"

D sat up straight as a button and began to speak thus: "Whatsoever my Crane could mean to me is rotted out by your constant flagrance in my presence. No. Don't sit up. Stand there like a shock of wheat and get trampled. Now I'm going to tell you once and for all, or maybe I won't. Maybe I'll start now and finish at some unforeseen time, or else not at all, the little you know and deserve. We'll begin by bisecting the problem, and I'll give you half. The other half I'll throw away. Can you be trusted? I'll have to. This is a quiz, but not really. My Crane is to me . . . I'll whisper it . . . my Crane is . . ."

R scampered out the door and met Emmie LaBelle who pointed into the sky. "Lookit," she said.

"I'm looking. I'm looking and I like it," R hollered. The Cranes were flying. R trundled back in to alert D, who had fallen into a funk. He led D out by the collar. "Now. Now get yours and let it go. Now's the time."

D tried to look up, without lifting his chin. What do you expect he saw? He slipped back into the room and made no more appearances, while R strolled out into the fragrance and wondered what had become of her. He made an easy pass around the lake and into the hills that were filthy with rhododendron. He had expected all the time that it wasn't winter, but maybe not. It's terrific up here, it's awful nice, he thought. He sipped from a babbling brook, and then licked his chops. Somewhere, he thought, was a different girl named Gertrude. By the time it was dark he was enlightened. He got back to the house and had to crane his neck to see D, who was still at the end of his rope painting the mirror yellow.

"I discussed the significance of your Crane," R said to D.

"It's none too soon. Now you can share my bliss," said D.

"Don't waste your precious gifts," R said, and sat down to write a novel.

D trickled down from the rope-top and stowed his paint can on his Crane. It was time to grate the horse-radish. D always believed that when your friends buckle down, the time is ripe to make hot condiments. R was penning his way to a life of his own in the age of comput-ers.

This has been the story of D and R. The ending is courageous, cryptic and predictable; but here comes the unexpected:

With his mind firmly established R stomped back to D's dimly lit residence. The bells from all around the city began to hush. R pushed D's till it hushed. D sidled up to the door and looked into the dim porchlight. R seemed to glow, but D didn't notice.

"You're just in time," D said breathlessly.

"In time for what?"

"To help me spell." D was sweating.

"Spell what?"

"Spindrift."

"Spindrift. What the fuck is spindrift?"

"Spell it."

"S," R commenced Shyly. "P," he Pontificated. "I," he Intoned. "N," he got Nervous. "I'm nervous," said R. "I can't move."

"Just go on. Go on," said D. "Don't stop. Just drift. Spell drift."

"D," he Drew a club from under his shirt. "R," he Raised the club above his head. "I." He Inched closer to D. "F." He Followed D's every motion carefully with his beadlike eyes. "T." He Tapped D on each shoulder.

"Look at what happened," D said, exhilarated, and they both gaped out there over the icy streetlamps at a happy hunting ground.

CHAPTER 14

--Oh, I left his lips slip under,
and then ... --And then? --That
was over. Good for me. I yipped--
The one on top needs to be
caustic.

These slap-ups here they hunch
spit plunge lick fuck belt puke and
burn. They don't just hang around
pretty like smallpots. They're
humaniferous, so what's your ploy?

He literally spelled his way to fame.

His very name was
a black mark against
his name.

Pious scandals, pious scandals.
Wait for the delivery. You can't
blurt out your qualifications like
that and expect an instant plush
reprisal.

 (continued on page 43)

MYTHOLOGY: OEDIPUS

So where's the big deal? I mean you screw your mother when you don't know who she is and maybe she's good so you do it again or if you're stupid you marry her; or maybe she's just boring like a lot of women, so you stop, or else you're really stupid. What's to put your eyes out about? Even if you know who she is, so what? As long as she's got what it takes, and you've got the urge, and she's got eyes, I'll tell you it's a sin if you don't. Only if she's a lazy hump, then you're out of your mind if you keep it up, and any mother who won't fuck like a demon for her own son isn't worthy of the name. What's the world about, anyway? I could tell you stories about my friends, stories I've heard, that would pop your eyes out of your head of their own free will. But I'm not going to tell you that kind of story yet, because I'm going to tell you about me, my story, which will bore you a little, except you can proba- bly see my missing eyes which create suspense, but not much. You can bet your sweet gezootskee this isn't one third as engrossing as the story of Two-Tongue Michael, Toilet Bowl Harry, or Jack Pushel.

This is a love story, and it proceeds as follows: I was born of very poor circumstances on the Lower East Side of New York and I spent the better part of my youth fighting and scuffling and rapping and hassling, and playing stick-ball, of course; but I knew that way down within myself there dwelt a simple country boy, a country boy who'd never seen a pig a horse a sheep, a cow a chicken a fowl a goat, but a country boy who knew he loved all that. It kept me going through eight knife-fights, a slice from a sharpened belt buckle, a busted head from a chain, seven stomped ribs, and not to mention a ruptured asshole from when I stole one of the Condor's chicks and they reamed me with a broomstick. I went through it all because I knew what was coming was the green grass and all the animals and a cool little stream and fresh food to eat and trees. Some day that would be it. Well, some day came and it was that. I got a job on a small dairy farm and I worked my ass off all through the haying season and after, mowing, turning and tetting, following the baler, throwing and load-ing sometimes till one in the morning if it looked like rain. Peacock was the name of my farmer, and he was in love with his Jersey cows, because they really are pretty, and you should have seen him one night the way I saw him, but that's another kind of story. He gave me my Sundays, and usually I'd hang around, relaxing, sleeping in the hay, reading "The Country Gentleman," and occasionally jerk-ing off. One Sunday along comes a beauty girl, or woman, as the case may be. She is such a beauty I roll off the hay-mow and land at her feet. "You're such a beauty," I say.

She, herself, was struck by me, because being a city boy flourishing in the country, I was sharper and looked like a whiz. We crawled back into the hay and engaged in a little rural-city interplay, to put it politely. I'll say this right now: A country girl, be she your mother or not, given all the obvious disadvantages of a small-time, country, rural life, will outball a city girl who has had all the city advantages, four times a night, and seven times in the afternoon, which is their specialty. Well, I walk her home, and her father (who as you probably guess is really my you-know-what), is very unhappy because a couple of his best milkers have dried up with mastitis.

Just the same he asks me jocularly, "Hey what is black and white, has four legs and you squeeze its teats twice a day?"

"You got me, Pops," I explain. "I don't know. What is black and white, has four legs, and you squeeze its teats twice a day?"

Well I never got an answer to that, and I still haven't doped it out, because the old man went out to do chores and me and his daughter went upstairs to, you know, exchange gametes. Anyway I married her after a proper period of courtship, and decided it was time to go visit the people I call my folks, because they brought me up. The Lower East Side didn't look so bad to a city boy who has just broken his ass on a farm. "Look," I said to my wife. "We can leave the country where it is and come down here for a while so I can be a poet. I feel poetry in my soul."

The people I call Mom and Dad embraced us and then stepped back to have a look. "You're such look-alikes," said Mom. "She's the spitting image of you and you're the spitting image of her. Just hold on a second, because we want to check something out." They were gone for a couple of hours, but that's all right because we always have something to do. When they got back we were just buttoning up.

"Listen," said the man I called Dad. "Never do that again, because you just fucked your real mother. We never said much about it, son, but you know we adopted you, and you're an adopted child, and we checked that she's your real mother, and you know you should never fuck your mother."

"Holy shit," I exclaimed, and looked at her. "I'll be a son of a bitch." Well I hustled into the bathroom and did the dumbest thing of my life, and I bet you couldn't match it. I put out my eyes with a Py-Co-Pay toothbrush, and that was no snap. I came out of the bathroom with bleeding eye-sockets and my wife-mother combination takes one look and says, "What a mess. You think I'm going to live with a blind poet? You think I'm going to hang around copying down poems? My Grandma said never trust a man who puts out his eyes because he probably killed his father. So goodby."

She left. There I was blind as shit without a wife or mother, and in my opinion it shouldn't happen to a mongoose. It's never worth it. I'll give you a piece of advice, and it won't cost you nothing. If you want to put out your eyes, you don't have to fuck your mother.

Now if you were a more careful listener I'd tell you a better story, about Four-Hose Milly. But you didn't even listen. In fact you were so inattentive I'm not even going to stamp your passport for you, so fuck off you freaky foreigner.

CHAPTER 16

He infabulated that art no more
don't have the scald, no malt-
beasts. I spake: Look. Where
have ever you been out of your
numb, spoon-filled cloist? Slip
up to my height and say that.

If I could just invent the steam
engine, then you'd see a return
to the good old days.

They call him fly-boy, but that's
an overstatement. You can play
the runt as well, and I'll wear
the outfit.

 (continued on page 43)

NINO

For the third time in that many days he got on the bus. This time he examined the seats and windows carefully, opening one window and looking at his hand through it to assure himself the glass was transparent. He saw his hand. The station agent told him the bus was going North, as did the driver, and many of the passengers whom he asked. They must have thought him peculiar for asking. One must have patience, he thought. He had learned during the war, when he was very young, and food was scarce, that the patient man endures hunger best. He applied the principle everywhere.

Many people told him that the new town where he had come to live by accident or choice, at the end of a gulf that fingered the desert with coral reefs and luxurious fish, was the end of the world, and perhaps that was true. "Better to call it the beginning of the world," he told them. They came to the rooms he rented in his small hostelry to escape, to make love and to have the sun. He was a fisherman.

The bus was a stranger matter. He had taken it two times

the two days previous and each time had noted the familiar landmarks of the desert pass his window as he headed North to the city. He would doze, and wake up near arrival, and step off the bus to find himself back there, where he had started. Most peculiar was that the circumstances didn't upset him. He easily went back to work as usual, rowing calmly out in the evening to check his nets. The next day he tried again. This was the third day.

At his side a dark-eyed girl with a long, heavy braid tried to keep from glancing at him, though it was clear she found him handsome. He was accustomed to that because women frequently came to him from the rooms he rented and in one way or another asked him to make love. That was one of his delights in staying there at the end, or the beginning of the world. This girl didn't neglect him, but he paid no attention, because he needed to concentrate on where he was going, which was North, to the city. He liked to think of the city as the place of light, because that was what he expected there. His life at home was passed during the daylight, whereas in the city, life turned around and he lived at night because of the luscious colored light there was, a visible feast at night. Darkness was darkness at home, and there was little he cared to do about it, a candle now and then, some feeble electricity.

It entertained him to think that the illusion he had of traveling the last two times he was on the bus had been done with lights, but he couldn't value himself so much to believe that someone would actually play this elaborate and costly trick on him. He would have been joyously flattered were it true because he was a humble man, living an obscure life. He had no doubt that such a thing with lights could be done by ingenious city people and that was why he checked the windows and looked carefully around the luggage racks and seats. The bus started moving.

"Are we moving?" he asked the girl.

She hadn't expected him to address her, so she nodded and shyly looked away.

"Are you headed for the city?" he asked.

"I'm from the city." She turned to face him. From the expression on her face one could think she had won a prize.

"Then you're going back," he finished.

The landmarks passed properly and quickly: the dry sulfur-wash, the blue plateau, the corrugated salt-marsh, lavender canyon. If it was a trick that was being played on him it was such an intricate practical joke that it would be rude of him to object. It seemed as complicated a joke as real life. The girl beside him was relaxed now, and each time he glanced at her she received his attention with a mellow smile. What could he be thinking? Certainly she couldn't be an actress hired for the role of *the girl who sits beside him*. Who could he think he was?

"I'm just a fisherman," he said to her.

"You sound like you're apologizing, why?" she asked.

"And I rent rooms to travelers." He didn't answer, but looked quickly back out the window. They were starting to climb, as they were supposed to, the motor of the bus winding down like a growling beast, and making him comment to himself, despite himself, "Good sound effects." If he weren't so preoccupied with the journey he could have paid more attention to the girl, who seemed lovable.

"Are you fishing well now?" she asked, and she looked at him with a kind, sympathetic gutsiness that made his hands want to touch her.

"For the last two years the catch has been poor, worse than ever. But I never worry about it. Everything changes." He looked at her. "I just haven't been able to get to the city." He almost explained it all to her, but decided to look at her instead.

Though he had all but dismissed the idea that a trick was being played on him, when the bus broke down near the phosphorous springs the thought that first crossed his mind was, "Well, this is a realistic touch." It was. A tire had blown and one of the shocks had broken in the rear. He got out to help repair it. The other passengers too got out and milled about the desert close to the bus, picking up and discarding stones. Suddenly it was as if a shower of sequins had fallen on the horizon when out of the white light around them seventeen men materialized aboard their camels, twirling their short spears like batons and singing brightly. All the passengers but the girl retreated to the bus. The tall, swarthy men, their robes shiny as polyester, rode slowly down to where the girl was squatting to examine stones, and they circled her there singing rounds that sounded like the music of people who worshiped something. He put down the wrench and walked into the middle of the ring of camels to stand beside the girl. Although he sensed that it was real danger they were in, it seemed absurdly made up to him, as if they were all, including himself and the girl, on a movie screen, done with lights. The light on the white stones of the desert was so strong that everything he saw seemed to dissolve in it, except the men. They were there, and they wanted her.

"I'm not afraid," she said to him. In fact, she wasn't. She was dancing from camel to camel, touching their noses. He noticed that she had pale soft skin and that her teeth were straight and white and set in four even rows. How had he come to be the one to defend her? He didn't have time to ask himself that question. The most radiant of the men, a baritone, moved his camel inside the ring and dismounted, his pajama leg slipping up to reveal the jewels set in his ankles. The baritone put his heavily ringed hand on the springy hair of the girl. Now was the time to act. He stiffened his long, pointed, Italianate hand and drove it like a spear into the breast of the camel, feeling around in there for the animal's heart which he grabbed hold of while it squirmed as if it were alive. He yanked it out and held it up before the face of the robed baritone. The animal sank as if its bones had melted. The man immediately drew a studded scimitar from under his robe and raised it, singing like a war-fiend. He raised the same stiff hand and brought its edge down on the robed shoulder, severing the cartilage, and causing the arm to flap like a decoration. The weapon dropped to the ground and he took it up.

"We're ready to rip," shouted the bus driver.

The camel-riders disappeared, singing into the harsh light from where they had appeared, and he heaved the scimitar after them, the light reflected off it making him shut his eyes.

"You must be so strong," she said.

"I must be. I never tried that before."

"You saved my life."

"An obligation, but a pleasure."

They were closer to the city, he could tell, because the landscape was turning greener and there was some farming. It was getting dark.

"You will have to pay for the heart of the camel," the girl said.

"Why should I have to pay for it?"

"Because that's their law."

"But what is the heart of a camel worth?"

"What, indeed."

The sun was down now. He saw through the driver's window a glow he knew was the city. This time he was getting there for sure.

"We're getting there," he said, almost touching her.

"What did you expect?" she laughed at him.

For the first time in these three trips he was awake as they entered the city. Light was on, and folks were moving about in it. People sat in the lighted cafés and sipped brightly colored drinks. Tramcars sparked, women shined. He would, he thought, have to find his hotel quickly, and get out and walk around. As soon as the bus pulled into the station he grabbed his satchel and went to the door. The city always made him feel puppyish. When the door opened he smelled the salt air. Other passengers seemed to have left by the rear door. He stepped off the bus. It has happened again. It was dark. He was home.

"Where are we?" he asked the driver, pretending to be confused.

"One way. You bought the ticket, didn't you?"

The driver was right. He had bought a one-way ticket, so where else could he be but there? It didn't even seem strange to him that it hadn't worked. He was back, and that was the end of it. Even his partner was waiting for him to tell him that they would have to work late because there was an unusually big catch in the nets, an unexpected tonnage of fish. They worked till long after midnight, and when he got home he made some coffee before bed. He guessed that was the last time for a while he would try to go to the city. The girl. He had been so anxious to get off the bus he hadn't even remembered to say goodby. She had said something about the heart of the camel. How would he pay for it? That was something he had done, all right. He had saved the girl. Just then there was a sound at the door, the knock of a female.

"I love you," said a voice that was there when he opened the door. He lit a candle that cast its glow on the face of the girl from the bus.

"Did you get here by bus?" he asked her.

"No. I hitched. It's easier," she said, and put herself in his arms.

"This is my house," he told her. "Treat is as your own." His name was Nino.

CHAPTER 12

This is the work of
genius and free speech.

Decorate the bedrooms of your heart
with the pennants of lust.

You look and find peas, peas and a Greek
barber, and the filly's Hohner (the surface tension is terrific), and a lot of
muslin. So you jerk off.

Sure I found my proper nook through the
placement service, and you can mention
my luck, but you won't squeeze joy from
an oyster.

Cholesterol, he said, cholesterol.
Consider what it does to the heart.
Without it who would ever have heard
of cholesterol. I'm not a doctor,
but I love my fats.

(continued on page 43) **117**

5 MYTHOLOGIES

MYTHOLOGY: NANCY AND SLUGGO

Nancy was the gayest shot in the West. He loved the boys the way other cowboys used to love the horse. He was lovable himself, and folks still love him, even after he's dead. All over the West the ne'er-do-wells feared Nancy's limp wrist. Even Sluggo, the terrible gulch-riding bandit, held Nancy in awe, though Nancy really had a crush on Sluggo and wanted to kiss him, or whatever. Nancy's biggest sin was what he wrote on bathroom walls; otherwise he was a boon to the West and a help to the sheriff. Few people knew he was gay because they thought he loved his horse, according to the script, and he did. His horse's name was Petal and Nancy braided its tail with ribbons, but he loved Sluggo better. Nancy's last name is Sweet. This is the story of how Sluggo caused the death of Nancy Sweet while Nancy was saving the town.

It happened on one of those days when Nancy was so busy shooting down desperados he could hardly pucker-up to puff the smoke off his gun-tips. The dreadful boys were falling left and right. "Oh, Doc," said Nancy. "This has been a trying day. All those pretty toughs I've had to do away with just because I'm hung up on the Code of the West. Oh they look so snuggly after they've done something naughty that it makes me want to spank their little saddle-worn 'derrières.' God help me."

"Sometimes you gotta do what you don't wanna do, so you do it and when you're finished doing it it's done, you did it," Doc philosophized. "Tell me something, though," he went on. "How come did you ever get a name like Nancy? Isn't that a girl . . ." Just then, Plebus Warneke, the last of the wholesome Warneke brothers, appeared in person from around the corner of the livery stable. He was the last of them, and the most wholesome of them all. Nancy spotted him first and said, "Bully sakes."

"Ya got my brothers, ya got my Uncle Pulp, Nancy Sweet, and now I'm gonna git you," Plebus Warneke rasped.

"Well, you desperados and banditos always make such a fuss, just come and get me. That's all you have to do." Nancy's hands bent like lilies over the gun-butts.

"Draw, Nancy Sweet," said Plebus Warneke in a voice that would curdle the blood of an ordinary man.

"Am I getting tired of this role," Nancy whispered. "Blam. Blam." He shouted, as usual, and the wholesome Warneke deflated like an orange bubble. "But he had such a sassy look to him." Nancy dolefully watched Doc declare him dead.

"He's dead," said Doc. "I don't know how you do it every time, but you do. About your name, though. How come your name is Nancy? Isn't that a . . ." But Nancy was gone, back to his room to give himself a facial.

Nobody knew the mysterious truth, but Plebus Warneke wasn't really the last of the Wholesome

Warnekes. There was Sluggo, the fearsome gulch-riding bandit, who was so rotten the Warnekes themselves had discarded him. He was worse than wholesome. He and Plebus had been born as Siamese twins, joined back to back at the buttocks, and they had been separated by an old Chinese surgeon called Yump. Plebus had got the bad blood, but Sluggo had got the worser. By a smart coincidence the following strange metabiological phenomenon occurred between them: They were left with mutual sensations in common. When Sluggo broke his leg, Plebus limped; when Plebus made love, Sluggo came. What happened when Nancy killed Plebus Warneke was that Sluggo, who was drinking rusty water in his hidden hideout blurted out "Yipe, I've been hit in my brother." He wrapped three lard sandwiches, saddled his horse Whiskey, and headed for town. The showdown was at hand.

"I love you, Nancy Sweet," said Stephanie Tutt as she massaged his cheeks. She was gorgeous, graceful, voluptuous, alluring, dynamic, sexy, sultry, courteous, friendly and rich. Everything a man could want in a woman. "I love you closer than sheep can graze the open range to anger the average cattleman and cause a range war," she purred.

"Ta Tee," said Nancy Sweet.

Just then the batwing doors of the saloon slapped open and the action froze and the faces turned and the voices whispered beneath their breath, "It's Sluggo, the horrible gulch-riding bandit."

"Show me the little boy's room, I gotta pee," boomed a voice that could stop tumbleweed dead-still in a high wind.

The bartender pointed a pallid index finger at the batwing doors of the men's lavatory. Sluggo stomped on in and everyone began again to carouse in a manner familiar to all Western fans. There was a message for Sluggo scratched on the wall above the piss trench. "Dear Sluggo, if you want a scrumptious blow-job, meet me out back in twenty minutes. N.S." Sluggo's eyes bugged out as he waggled the last drops off. "So that's the varmint I gotta git," he snarled.

"Nancy. Nancy." There was a knock on Stephanie Tutt's door and the little man busted in. "Sluggo, the hideous gulch-riding bandit just walked in through the batwing doors and he's pluggin' to git you."

"Oh dear," Nancy sighed. "It's like a dream come true. Now sheriff, don't fret your little chestnuts none. Just let me handle him, sweetie." Nancy winked at the sheriff and hustled him back out the door. He hadn't a moment to spare.

"Nancy. Nancy," said Stephanie Tutt weepingly. "I'm so afraid for you. Hide in my closet. Hide in my trunk. Hide under the bed. Hide in the window seat. Hide behind the door. That Sluggo, the horrendous gulch-riding bandit, is the most wanted man in the Western Territory."

"Of course he is, Steph; and who do you think wants him the most?" Nancy wiped off the remainder of his cold cream and examined his pores in the mirror. He was ready for action. "We haven't a moment to lose, Steph dear," he said resolutely. "Get out the lavender satin, the frilly one with décolleté, and that modest bustle, a pair of black mesh hose with the sequinny garters, the ultratight corset (you'll have to bind me) and those lacy net furry little slippers." Stephanie Tutt hustled around like a personal maid while Nancy dressed himself, applying lip rouge and eyeshadow at the last.

"How does it look? Nancy asked.

"It looks weird, Nance," Stephanie laughed. "But even so I adore you. Aren't you going to carry a gun?"

"Stephanie, my dear," said Nancy, raising his bare right shoulder. "You know I always carry a gun." Nancy Sweet swished out the door.

He gracefully descended the long stairway catching the whistles and catcalls and hurling them back as kisses. He left through a rear door, lifted his skirts, and tiptoed around back to where he knew Sluggo would be waiting. There was Sluggo all right, glowing with a gray light.

"Hi there," Nancy breathed huskily.

"Honey, I ain't got time for no poodle petting," Sluggo quipped. "I come here to kill a mizzuble varmint."

"You came here because of the message above the pissoir, and you know it, snookums." Nancy Sweet moved close to Sluggo so they were nearly rubbing thighs.

"How do you know about messages in pissers?"

Nancy Sweet raised a painted eyebrow. "It was my message, little loose-pants."

"Your message?" The dawn slowly rose on the visage of Sluggo. "Then you're the Nancy Sweet did in Plebus, my Siamese twin brother, my other brothers, my Uncle Pulp."

"The very same," Nancy curtseyed, and then lifted his skirts to reveal the gun on his garter.

"Though I hold you in awe I've gotta have it out with you, Nancy Sweet. I'm obliged to. And I never had it out with a woman before."

"How you do talk, Sluggo Warneke. What on earth makes you call me a woman?" Nancy gave him his coyest smile. "And besides, you never let anyone know you were one of the wholesome Warneke brothers. You were always worse than wholesome. You were straight arrow, clean-cut as apple pie. Now let's just forget all the enmity and have it out, as you put it. Snuggle a little, Sluggo,"

"Why you queer faggot Commie queer. You homosexual," Sluggo roared and snorted and waved his six-shooter in the air.

"Oh my," said Nancy Sweet. "How repetitive and boring is the Code of the West." They both let hot lead fly, and being an equal match killed each other to death. Watching from his window the Chinese surgeon called Yump slowly cried and smoked. Folks watched Doc pronounce Sluggo dead and then moved to the still-breathing form of the fastest ex-gun in the West. "Doc," Nancy said, "would you put my feet in my boots so I can die that way?" Doc yanked the boots on. "You're a sweetheart," were Nancy Sweet's last words before he died.

"What I still can't git," said Doc, turning to the little sheriff, "why was his name Nancy, isn't that a . . ." But Doc stopped because he could see the sheriff was crying. Stephanie Tutt was crying too.

"His life was like a fairy tale of the Old West," she peeped.

CHAPTER 23

"You spit lucky." Some cherubs
held up the bedlamp. Riff raff.
Just then we noticed his snorkel
was ablaze.

If you come over this evening
bring the endless butt-jokes and
spoofs, and don't forget your
goggles while I decide. Find
Hudsonberger.

Applause or no applause
I bring you the fish.

Respectability is no substitute for
madness.

 (continued on page 43)

MYTHOLOGY: GANDHI

Let us begin our discussion with a consideration of the worm, who merely starts and ends his rounds in the recesses of the earth, sometimes surfacing, sometimes not, munching both top and bottom soil, most unlike the potato bug. He is a worm. His name is Gandhi. He reproduces in a wormlike fashion and his conversation is most wormlike, as is his dress. Since his total length is stretched along the ground when he is on the surface, and all of it makes a little wormy track, Gandhi could be vulnerable to squishing if people walked on the ground around the domain of his rampancy. That is why the feet of people never touch the ground, a phenomenon that has never before been adequately explained. Of course you've noticed that if you shove a human he generally tends to go off anywhere from twenty-five to sixty feet in a direction continuous with the direction of the thrust, because only the slight braking influence of the atmosphere slows him down. This process is known as "shoving a human around," whereas Gandhi would say, "You can't shove me around," and we observe that it is true. You can't push a worm around. He'll fold up, knot, twist away or dive back into his hole. This "shoving a human around" is peculiar to humans, and Gandhi has much to say on the subject, not the least of which is his tract on the absurdity of human war, where the phrase "human flesh is scattered like stones" was first coined.

Gandhi himself has a kind of humility, but not as a result of his wormitude, as is often thought, though that too is spectacular. He has humility as an onion has layers. It is commonly thought, you see, that worms are merely good for gardens, and Gandhi does nothing to quell this rumor. It suits his mysterious purposes, whatever they are. It is often told that they chomp around the roots of the various legumes and tubers and vegetables, imbibing the commonplace soil, churning it through their wormlike interiors, and exuding behind themselves an exceedingly nutritious form of nitrogenous worm faeces. The various plants gobble that up through their root fibres, drawing out nutritious minerals and vitamins, and turning themselves into our favorite Brussels Sprout, Okra or Cauliflower, as fatuous as it all seems. Gandhi is quite happy that we take in that theory, while he carries on the work that really pleases him. It represents, at least, some kind of diminutive parallel to what we have recently discovered the worm is really up to: this idea that the humans drift around planting this or that, and adding this or that to the soil, while the real work is done below by Gandhi. Such a morbid idea quakes the intellect. The intellect is what we have come to suspect Gandhi is about, and we have been able only to begin to describe the extent of his influence, as far as vanity will permit. We have recently been willing to admit, of course, the influence of what we call "diet" on our mental capacities. Spinach, carrots, snow peapods, have long been called, colloquially, our brain food, whereas it has been recognized that the common beefsteak, pork chop, or leg of lamb has its greatest influence on human musculature. The extent of vegetable influence on so-called conscious human experience has never before been examined, nor has the area of its specificity been determined. We have just begun to crack the surface, and since digging up the new Gandhi theory our progress has been remarkable. Though we don't know yet all the tricks Gandhi has up his sleeve under there, we can generally sketch the outline, and will do so, foregoing technical details, to make it clear as possible to the human. Gandhi's real work below, as far as we can tell so far, produces a kind of thought energy, a far more significant form of production than the mere nutrition we had previously attributed to him. What is even more remarkable is that as the evidence mounts we find that he has a way of transporting quantities of this actual "brain food" through the roots of plants to the human gray matter, disguised, somehow, as common nutritive value. Whereas human writing is most generally accomplished through the pen, pencil, typewriter or somesuch, Gandhi accomplishes his exposition more or less viscerally, and as far as can be ascertained it must be communicated through the roots to the edibles in a kind of charged, microscopic alphabet soup, elaborately ordered and pro-grammed. The human, consuming this communication through potatoes or string beans or broccoli becomes thus informed.

We have found that these programs, the information communicated, are quite extensive—though we haven't yet determined just how so, but it seems that frequently the recipients of a certain balance of this nutrition tend to produce benign and edifying books. This is the most satisfactory explanation thus far for the phenomenon humans call inspiration, though it was mistakenly thought for a long time that something divine or female was the cause, whereas now it is clearly shown that so-called inspiration is nothing more than the dictation out of Gandhi's tummy. Though by present methods we can't determine Gandhi's age, we have evidence of his track at least as far back as the Book of Mormon, the Koran, the common Bible, and fainter but convincing evidence of his influence on the I Ching and the Vedas. One provocative theory, that we shall just mention here in passing, finds cryptogrammatic evidence of the name of Gandhi in the word Socrates, seeming to indicate that Plato too was informed by the worm. In technologically advanced human habitations an environment inimical to Gandhi is created, and a totally human phenomenon is caused in those advanced and powerful nations that we can call "hideous stupidity," a condition one detects immediately in the statements, writings, and policies created by the leaders of, let us say, overfed but undernourished peoples that tend to the state of Post-Gandhian and, therefore, formless alphabet soup.

We must still account for the gap there seems to be between Gandhian intelligence and human action, and the clue we are following now is the phenomenon we described at the opening of this discourse. The wisdom of the worm is of the earth. Human action is exaggerated by the gap between the earth and the sole of the foot. It is a gap, we have seen, necessary for Gandhian survival, but is widening, unfortunately, out of reach, and as it widens the possibility of the efficacy of Gandhian wisdom diminishes. So it goes. We'll keep a sharp lookout for further developments. As it is, we can only learn what we learn and hope for the best.

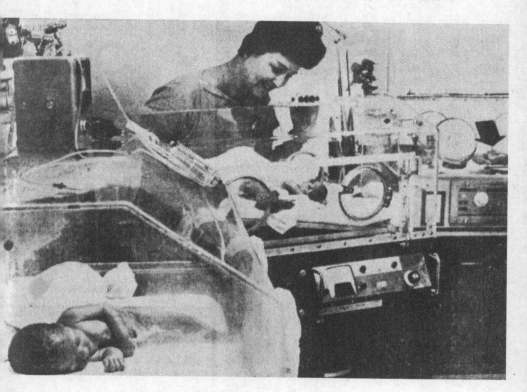

CHAPTER 15

Hi cupcake

Damn this awful lambfat.
Can't you stop painting
for one minute?

Wait under the boardwalk for the
kickoff event. No, being an artist
is not enough. There has to be a
flip side.

 (continued on page 43)

MYTHOLOGY: DICKENS

"It used to be, 'hands off the blues and the yellows, Martha.' And I didn't think that was so bad, but things have turned for the worst since then and they aren't any better, not even at lunchtime. I can't spell anymore. My heart feels like it's three inches above my head, and the elevator doesn't even work. I never started, and he expects me to stop, so what's the use? Work and work and he gets home and clobbers everything with his blundering personality which couldn't dope out a nuance if it was slapped in his face. What sounds do words make? Go on. He tells me to go on and points his finger and expects me to hop on it. Maybe for him it's easy when he does his breathing exercises and the rhythm cycle he bought when I can't afford a cup of hot chocolate. He calls me his trained flea just because it itches when I go by. I feel like a whore out of it. In the mirror I say to myself, 'You whore,' and then I relax and dress up funny. But he hasn't shown a puff of affection since six days ago last Wednesday a month. Is this what you call reality? The butt end of my string is on its way, so help me. Help me."

Dickens stared through her at the wall behind which was covered with glowing wrappers, and he chortled deep and slow. She clutched her rucksack and sat with her mouth ajar because it was impressive to see him in the flesh. Many weary miles over the prickly deserts over the marshy swamps over the horny mountains she had made her pilgrimage to confer with the Dickens. Others went by jet or boat or train or used the special Dickens bus service, and no one found it disappointing. His cave, first of all, wasn't of the commonplace natural type found elsewhere, but it was a glittering artificial he had come upon in those years he had been wandering the wastes and wilderness. It was well preserved in what must have been a sprawling city of the ancients, near a huge body of water that is unexplored because still radiating. Strange monuments stand in the region as testimony to whatnot, and those who dare to dig can find things. This all sounds to the average person like hocus-pocus science fiction, but it's the realistic truth as far as can be told, and it's the mystery that makes it such hot stuff. People have come for generations in time of trial to see the Dickens.

The Dickens squinted at the woman over his quill, the plume of which he twisted in his bonelike fingers, and he rubbed his pointy chin and plucked a hair from his ear which grew like thistle-fur. He placed this along with the ingredients the woman had brought in the imitation stone lamp. Then he dipped the quill and made a few entries in his ledger. The woman closed her eyes, better to soak in what he was about to say. "Just look for the silver lining, whenever clouds appear into view," he said cryptically. He lit the offering in the lamp and the room filled with the sound of ukuleles. Dickens took the woman's hand, placed it on his desk, and rapped the knuckles seven times with a ruler he took from the scabbard at his side. She then asked him for his last words and he drew in a deep breath that seemed to be his last, and his boney cheeks turned the color of Nebraska on the map. "Pack your coat," his voice creaked, "and get your hat, leave your worries on the doorstep." He swooped into a trance as he spoke. "Just direct your feet, to the sunny side of the street. Tell no one what I have said here," he admonished her, as he does everyone.

The woman left the Dickens with a new lease on life. She did everything carefully according to his instructions, and died three years later of a peptic ulcer, though happily not in midwinter as she had always feared, but on a glorious summer day when she was swimming and had been dragged under by the lecher of the deep, a turn of fate for which she thanked the Dickens eternally.

Dickens signaled for the next pilgrim and hacked consumptively into a blue handkerchief.

". . . black warts on his neck and none on mine . . . turn a page, he turns it back . . . I don't drink but he's always polluted . . . and at sleep he'll be nibbling on my ear because he's homosexual and I'm not."

The Dickens stared through the two-headed man at the wall behind, and he chortled deep and slow. The two-headed man sat back with his mouths ajar and clutched their rucksack. The Dickens went through the usual ritual as if it were for the first time. "Just look for the silver lining whenever clouds appear into view," he intoned. "And remember that two heads are better than one."

The two-headed man guffawed with laughters. The Dickens made a last entry in his ledger, and then stood up straight looking angry. Then he pulled off his smock, revealing the creamy breasts of a young woman and a blushing abdomen. He lifted his face off as if it were a rubber mask, revealing such a perfect creature you would think this was a different story. Dickens then stepped out from behind his (her) desk and took the arm of the two-headed man and headed naked as a piglet down Hollywood Boulevard without even a toodleoo for the staff. "What the Dickens," they cried. The nude Dickens was immediately discovered by an ensorcelled talent scout and made into a star overnight. "Goodby, reading public," was the last entry in the ledger.

CHAPTER 9

You are only as good
as your shadow thinks.

She was slender as that antenna across
the glen--over there, where they cleared
the birches. That's enough. Line up.
Eyes shut.

Music is one of the attractions, but that's.
not the difficult adjustment to make.
There's the bend, the entrance, the slope.
Someone coughs.

Their tendency is to scatter at the whistle,
leaving the next shift to cope with a tacky
scum. That's the time to filch the
choicest for yourself, and I won't tell more.

Muck. Muck was there, and perfume and
riboflavin. I corraled the genius and asked
his conditions. Now I can tour the Finger
Lakes at will.

   (continued on page 43)

MYTHOLOGY: MANDRAKE

The little man sat on a bench in the personnel office of the mill. The time was ripe for revolution. Beside him sat a huge purple cohort called Lothar. He never wore a shirt and had muscles to bulge. The little man was not the kind of little man you could call small. He looked tough, like one of those aggressive little men you know can whip anyone twice his size, although this little man was smaller than that. When the secretary called the little man for his interview the purple one stood up to follow him in. He was twice the size. The little man sat down in a straight-backed chair beside the desk and the purple one took a space up beside him and folded his arms over his chest.

"Name?" the interviewer asked without a pause.

"Mandrake," said the little man.

"Haw. Haw." said the interviewer. "The magician." He gasped when he spied Lothar at his post. "Who's the nigger?"

"He's not a nigger. The man is purple. His name is

Lothar."

"Well, who wants the job? You? Or does he?"

"I'm applying for the job."

"Does he have to be here when I'm interviewing you?"

"It doesn't make any difference."

"Wait outside," he said to Lothar, who was huge and purple.

"I mean it doesn't make any difference when he stays here. It will make a difference if he leaves."

The interviewer slid away from his desk on the rolling chair and rolled across the painted cement floor. He took down the picture of two Hamburg Beer-Hounds, pushed off the wall, and rolled back to the desk. They all listened with interest to his beer-hound stories and his recording of their gleeful barks.

"All right," the interview began. "You got any phys-ical disabilities or you ever been in the hatch?"

"Yes."

"You ever worked in a mill before?"

"Never."

The little man got a job in the mill.

When the foreman asked who the nigger was, Man-drake explained that he was purple and his name was Lothar. "Haw. Haw," the foreman smirked. "And you're Mandrake the Magician."

"My name is Mandrake."

The foreman was a big man but he had very few muscles though he was strong but probably not as strong as Lothar looked. He saw Mandrake's name on the sheet, but not Lothar's.

"Blow, Nigger," he said.

"You can see that he's purple," interceded the little man.

"Does it make a difference that he stays here?"

"No."

"Goodby, Purple."

"No difference if he stays here, but it makes a difference if he goes."

"Haw," the foreman spoke up, and he sat down on a bench, rolled up his cuff, and showed them his wooden leg. "I save lint in a box at home," he said.

He sent the little man over to an idle stone crusher with a huge heap of ore beside it. The little man began in lightning swift time to be skilled in the mill. His pace was prophetic. After an hour's practice he could get more board feet out of a sack of superfine than any man alive or in recorded folklore. All this time the purple man stood by with his purple muscles extant, especially on his arms that were folded over his chest.

Other men in the mill had three reasons to resent the little one and his purple cohort, at which point the little man worked even more assiduously, defying the hourglass. Then something happened that warped the minds of youth, at which moment the little man was transferred to the rock crusher as a precautionary measure. Then came the incident that capped it all off, after which the little man labored while his purple companion stood beside him with arms folded over his chest. Then, after things seemed to have just settled back into a reasonable routine, it recommenced with undreamed-of consequences. Then the lunch whistle blew. It was time for lunch. The little man offered some of his scant lunch pail to his purple friend. The purple friend refused, turning his head from side to side and sniffing the air. All hell broke loose.

After that, lunch was over and the little man was transferred to the rock crusher. The unbearable noise was unthinkable so he sang instead such tunes as mothers sing to their laundry after the children are finally grown.

The other men in the mill fell asleep and Mandrake cased the joint and just as he had suspected the worst of his suspicions was justified. He became very quiet when the men started waking up. Just then Jeb the gouge-operator approached the static Lothar with his racial hang-ups. "Nigger, Nigger, Nigger, Nigger, Nigger, Nigger, Nigger," he insisted.

"Not Nigger, purple," the little man patiently reiterated. "Lothar is his name."

"Haw. Haw. Haw. And you are Mandrake out of the comic strip."

"The name *is* Mandrake, as a matter of fact."

At that moment the mill filled with an ominous scent of lilac. Someone slipped Lothar a sleeping potion. They clubbed Mandrake with a toolbox full of a wine-colored wax that smells like a pussycat smells to a tom-cat just before she goes into heat, and then they bound him with long strips of inner tube the color of damp grass after it is nearly dry. He began to giggle when he saw Lothar carried off in another direction.

"At last I'm free," he burbled. "I'm free. I'm free."

The mill men tumbled back in surprise when Mandrake snapped the rubber as if it were plastic and began to hobble around in the strange victory dance of his cult. At that moment the dreadful whistle unexpectedly sounded and the foreman shouted, "Quitting time." The purple one hustled across the mill floor and beat everybody up. Mandrake and he quickly captured the villainous foreman, and grabbed each executive as he corruptly left his office, and they piled them like laundered shirts into a nearby bus bound for Peekskill. "We promise," they barked like capitalist pigs, as their bus sped off.

The next day heralded the dawn of a new era of socialist reform.

CHAPTER 11

If society hadn't given up on me
where would I be today?

It's balance. One takes a chance
with a hair-style, and suddenly it's
in the wind. The family was not
stingy, but muscles is the last
straw. Nevertheless, I'm happy
to see you, Scotch.

To me he's a something to hang on to,
like a clipboard. I don't mean to
insult the old station at all, but I
never know where I'm at. I consider
myself a crisp fuck--eight men have
called me sensual--but he just
snaps like a rooster.

 (continued on page 43)

MYTHOLOGY: ACHILLES

The girls would love to like Achilles for what he is, but they can't because he is the kind of man you have to love or leave. Therefore they don't leave him, but they don't love him either. For this reason Achilles frequently rides the subways, and is known as Achilles in the Tube, or Turnstile Achilles or merely Achilles. For those of you who don't understand the subway the following will serve as an exposition: You can recognize Achilles *tout de suite* because he wears no coat in the winter in the subway and in the summer he doesn't sweat but he always carries a package. The subway has just enough room in the summer for people and sweat, and the same amount of room in the winter for people in their coats, except for Achilles, who doesn't wear his coat, but there isn't room for him anyway, though he gets on just the same. Crushed up against him was a patient in conference with her Reichian analyst. They conversed not as doctor and patient but as serious people. "Fear not masturbation nor the pleasure gained therefrom." The knuckles of Achilles of the hand that gripped the package sunk into the woolly buttock of another. He couldn't determine whose the buttock was he was pressing in close quarters. Across the car he spotted the face of a woman whom he didn't recognize and he wished that hers was the gluteus he had garnered. At home that night he had a dream about her.

Achilles' wife was tender and loving but she left him because she loved him and the woman who lived with him didn't love him though she told him the opposite and threatened to leave him. In his dream he hopped on the subway and saw the face of the woman whom he didn't recognize. "Fear not masturbation nor the pleasure gained therefrom," she warbled like a sparrow. He rubbed his hand along the buttock he was pressing and noticed that his package was gone, and to top it off the Reichian analyst, whose indecipherable grin he couldn't figure out, was scrutinizing his visage. When the train cleared out at 125th Street he noticed that the analyst wore no pants but had Achilles' box deftly placed over that through which he did number one. "What a funny dream I'm having," he said to the locket that held a snapshot of his Uncle Charlie. Then Achilles woke up and decided never again to ride the subways. Instead he went to face his boss and demand a raise.

On his way to the office he met a man who offered to trade the five magic beans he possessed for the Achilles package. Though Achilles said he no longer had the package the deal was on anyway and Achilles arrived at his office with the five beans. Lucy, the secretary, boiled them in the coffee pot and when he found them to be tasteless he decided to quit his job. By then the streets were full of the unemployed. It was late August, and the tension in the ghettos made the wealthy neighborhoods seem relaxed by comparison. But it was an uneasy truce with people milling on street corners and holding up their hats. "It's a matter of broken-field running and the appreciation of bebop." Achilles overheard one beardless man's remark. He felt he should explain to everyone how easy it was to pick up a stone. If everyone had a stone in his hand he could stand on a corner with a stone in his hand. Suddenly a bus pulled up right in front and he hopped it. When he woke up he was eight blocks away. People were standing on these corners with stones in their hands and a chill crawled up their spines. Achilles had forgotten how to spit three boxes, how to whistle with two fingers, and how to fake out the boss of the candy store. When he saw the subway entrance he decided to lie low. A cabin by the sea was where he did that, where choice edible seaweed washed up on the shore. As pleasant as he found all the splashing it wasn't his cup of tea and when he got back he found the city had been changed. The unemployed had been employed and they all hated it. What was he to do? The young played stickball on the block. The boys played stickball on the street. "Aren't you ashamed of yourself?" asked a woman in passing. Achilles was ashamed of himself but it didn't help. He hiked from 243rd Street to the Battery without a result. It was there that he met the Philosopher of the Barges. Too tired, and yet too excited; too weak, and yet overcome with his new-found power, Achilles was at his wit's end. He could see the body of a woman floating in the harbor. It bobbed on the shallow waves like an open bottle. "You should walk back to 243rd Street," said Mr. Philosopher. Achilles knew he would have to face a challenge. At the halfway point he met a blind old man who wouldn't give him the time of day. When the fight started he hurt his foot and limped around cheering. What had become of his home and his family? What of his friends? What of the old teacher who taught him in school? He finally got into a fight with a guy who could kick the shit out of him when all of a sudden, to everyone's chagrin, the ghetto conditions improved and the fighting stopped, leaving Achilles with a case of empties. The last straw broke the camel's back, but not Achilles'. From out of the blue the woman whom he didn't recognize landed on top of him, foiled in her suicide attempt. At first she was peeved, but then she recognized the man whom she didn't recognize. That was when Achilles turned on the transistor and listened to Bo Diddley. "Never leave me," he said. "I'll never love you," she retorted. He picked her up softly in his arms and carried her like a poster down the subway steps. Several words of advice were printed on the walls and may they always be a lesson to us. There they sat: Achilles and the woman whom he didn't recognize. She wrapped a new package for him and he rubbed knuckles on her buttock. When the train came Achilles shut off the radio and got aboard, but she didn't because she had to meet her girl friend uptown. They waved goodby and were happy forever.

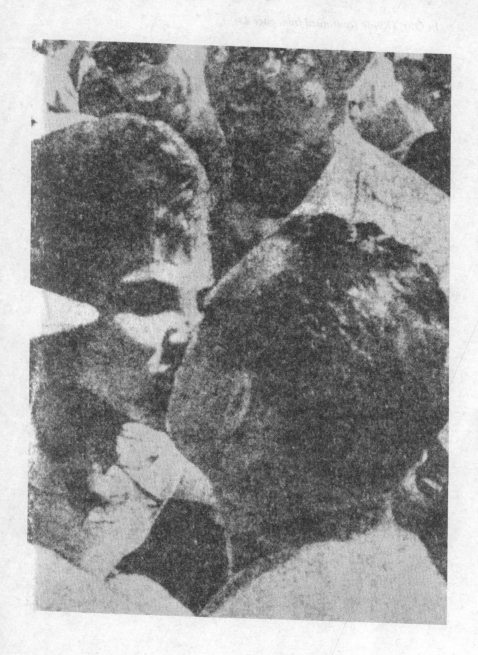

CHAPTER 21

It's done with tape, furs, jello, #8
needles, a fire escape, and spurs.
Don't stand on it too long or
others will hear you. At 4:30, relax.

If television were good for the eyes
I wouldn't have to write so pleasantly.

defend your liver

The place was thick with empty talk
when with a gasp the curtain rose
and for seventeen trouble-free hours
they gaped at a buttery light.

6 HAIKU

tell what she has planned because she has made it her secret
I resolve that I love her and therefore I oppose the war
my plea is anemic   when she smiles I feel the steam of the
sea   if I could know what my love means I would speak of
it frequently but hobbles   the fine moments come when I
manage to oppose the war with my wit   here in her house
the room lists slowly from one side to the next as if we are
at sea   she believes in confusion because it makes the world
rich   I need to understand what she means   she explains
that she feels too woozy at sea to pursue questions   no she is
not at sea   she isn't prepared yet to let me turn from the wall
that I face while she prepares   who knows what it is   I need
her to be there when I start to explain myself   I mean I hear
gulls   I hear gulls I say   you have a mighty ear she re-
sponds   that wasn't a gentle remark   was it patronizing
she might have touched me   my eyes are sick of the wall but

with her I hold this burden of patience   I love to watch her
while she sleeps and think of things I need to tell her   love
in me is whatever I cannot say when she is awake   blank as
this wall   I push the language   love is this blank wall I
say   that so she mumbles   she could be sleeping   I'm about
to turn around I say   don't she says you will be sorry   how
can she be so sweetly arrogant   how do I always respond
as if disciplined   the word discipline enrages me   I rotate
from the wall and speak thus   I am a militant and have
much to do you make me stare at this wall what is so important that I must be bound by you if you need something done
about the war you must not keep me staring at the wall   you
do nothing   she has been staring at my back throughout
this   I stand up and speak   I won't stare at your goddamn
wall there is a war and we are beasts yes and our unmention-
able pleasure is to murder torture burn our brothers while I
stare at this wall and the hideous war is unspeakable and I
have to do something   I lift my fists in front of my face and
stop talking   her smile swims away   now you have spoiled
it she says

always comes different   I mean to tell her about the war but
she has found something of her own to keep in her hair to
distract me   I get to her and she nabs my voice before I can
say I am distressed   I must be lying about the war   whom
can I query about the pain   it comes   I hear the whining
fins and they don't sound bad   even to mention the war to
her would be second rate   has she enough quality of darkness to cope with honest appraisals   not mine you remember
     I eat up descriptions of the sounds of war   when I tell her
that she folds over like the envelope in my pocket if I could

remember the address if I could remember the questions if
I could recognize the answers I would mail in my protest
something goofy in her eyes like thirst makes me mute   are
these distractions plausible   I am driven off when she snarls
if I reach for the way   we are all dying in the war and I need
some time to mention it   on the other hand she brings up
the children she has to raise   I try to slip the war up onto
the shoulders of that issue   the children you need to raise
are in danger   what danger she asks   in danger of death
from war   is that death different from any other   that death
is a tyrannous waste   do you suggest I don't have the children I want to raise   I want to say that I understand the
various sufferings of the many peoples suffering in the world
and though I am comfortable I have compassion   a smile
glides over her lips like the reflection of wavelets on a stone
wall

her mind in tomatoes and I have a load on my tongue   who
knows what I see in myself and here it comes   mass murder
civilian population defoliation starvation neo-nazis   eyes is
one of her specialties   lazy dog fragmentation bombs muti-
late civilian populations   another the lips   favorable kill
ratio   her cheeks her swell ears   infants scorched war zone
c napalm   that word napalm softens up her smile   she says
I miss tomatoes she throws some of it some of her hair back
of her shoulder   napalm   that word again from my mouth
is kissiform   I need to get going about the war   palms of
her hands on her thighs   she needs to open spaces where the
answers can grope   I must tell some truth about the war
napalm   I try the word on my mouth but it never works
napalm is   she steps nearer to me through the honey of that

sound   hideous   she says I miss having the plants and the
summer when I eat tomatoes nothing else   napalm   that
sound in the lingo of a happy island means love   n'palm   I
slip across the rug to see if she can help me to some of the
language I approximately feel   napalm again and that is
what I am closing in on her   napalm napalm   something
in that noise undresses us   her clothes burst like tomatoes
dropped on the floor   I would concentrate on my opposition
to the war   her satin briefies flick off her ankles and wiggle
like automatic rounds in the dirt   the air has nerves   everything is fine for us and napalm says itself out of my mouth
become our special way to speak   she sucks my cheek as if
it is ripe   I know I must be lying what I say about the war
   napalm that sound is my face on her thigh and she is whispering a something I should listen   napalm   I separate her
lips where they are soft they are salt   I put my tongue   the
tongue I need to speak against the terror it is not sweet
around my tongue but it soaks my voice in answering and I
put my mouth there to the hot stirring and blow into its
roominess back of the lips and lift my face away to listen
napalm napalm napalm it answers in soft bleating flatulence
   I scrape the sweat from my brow with the edge of a pocket
mirror   what runs down my image there looks
like tears

IV

don't come my way with your sexual fantasies when there's
a war happening is what she should be telling   one of those
has to keep one of me on the narrow gauge   war mass freak-
out carnage blood rite romp of paranoid fat american asses
squat over tiny spoonful country phhhhwwwwwwwaaaa-
hhhhh   the sound of our war   there is the scandal of it all

this delicious talk about the war   helpful as an overnight hike   words come up my throat like that relax off my lips I nip them off into syllables   I want to say what I feel and she unlocks the wrong books   here's her list the unplanted garden the unconceived family the little hideout in a splotch of woods her clubfoot hopes   my list is troubled and stupid and you know what it is   I want to say what I feel about the war I like it so much   just think of all those people being maimed for you and dying and screaming and with their babies rolling around in the rice paddies in blood   there's my happiness   do I mean what I say   I said I can't say what I mean   I can't mean what I mean   it sounds comfy to me all those little yellows snoozing on the conscience of america   such a place to rest as roomy as Lincoln Center   one of the american boys nipped by snipers in the woods is worth more than six of the others   proof isn't necessary   I'd love to carry a gun around myself if I could learn how to shoot they call what you squeeze the trigger   you squeeze it   I could get all duded up to do that   not a word yet from her and she would let me work out this tack forever with her snow peas on her mind or something   I love to devastate the oriental races I fly over them in the jungly places in the mountain places in the plains when the floods where they hide the little yellow you know whos and drop on them the you know what   phhhwwwwwwwaaaahhhhh   isn't this exhausting   think of the poor boys who actually have to do all that   it must wear them down   it tires me just to have to say something while she digs her furrows or whatever   oh well I guess I'll hurry to the frozen food counter and get something frozen for dinner   we'll have a deepfreeze there she said something   what was that   a deepfreeze to freeze up my garden in so we can have an all-winter garden selection for ourselves   they stock where I go a nice variety there of frozen peas frozen carrots frozen beans frozen peas and car-

rots frozen chicory frozen succotash frozen spinach frozen
kale frozen okra frozen spuds frozen collards frozen baby
limas frozen black-eyed peas and many frozen others as well
as delicious frozen combination dinners and many frozen
gourmet stuff   I wish it were easy as this to tell the truth
about the war   could I be a deserter of the cause you may be
chilled in my tub of atrocities

so so so so   intercourse at a dead minimum and then it is
time to lay it on the line about the war   she slaps her heel
on the spade and pops it in to the loamy underfoot   I can't
feel it what you feel about the war the way you look at me or
almost anything she speaks   now's the time to blow something up I raise my fists and am the letter Y   you see what I
mean I can't she whimpers   why do you say that you can't
just think tough   it's not up to me I can't think that way and
besides I'm colored she upends a spadeful of the shiny black
    I take my usual three steps back   that's the cake taker
what she says   she has got the white face she has got the
white hands a little bit of the white ankle I can see   some
streaks of garden grime but never was she otherwise than I
have been seeing her white all the time I have gone to her   I
say what sort of double-talk and begin to circle her slowly   I
can't think she says the way you think about the war   you
said something else   I said I am colored and you're forty-
three feet tall   I am not forty-three feet tall   and you are
not colored   does it make a difference to you that I am colored   it makes not a bit of difference to me but you are not
colored   it sounds to me like it makes a difference to you so
I'm colored and I'm colored and I'm colored and this dilemma began when she asked me to come submit to an ex-

planation of her cause which has always been her garden
just look at yourself and then say if you are colored   she
won't gamble a look   don't be silly I know I'm colored she
says   your skin is white very white I grab her wrist to demonstrate her hand to her   you look just on the surface of
things she turns her head   white lady white   there's more
than that to it   what more to it you don't even talk colored
   do you think we are all uneducated country darkies who
say yassuh constantly and play the juice harp some of us
are clothed in western culture for better or worse   I sneak
back to the barrels and squat there watching the carnivorous
birds   she is planting tomatoes as usual   several questions
amble through my mind and no stop to it   was Ho Chi
Minh anti-semitic can Israelis learn manners are Russians
normal can we find the way out is China a longshot   getting
to the surface of things is the process of skimming crud off
the top and in this situation the top is never apparent   I see
her tired of gardening and lead her into the room of mirrors
   are you sure you aren't a yellow oriental I put in her ear
she stares at the mirrored wall   today I planted many kinds
of the tomato the fireball the long Italian the yellow tomato
the succulent beef the bitsy cherry tomato yellow and red and
one other which is the mystery tomato in my garden   why
won't you answer my question   what question   if you are
a yellow oriental   that is not a question you are stupid look
at me do I look oriental   you don't look colored either   I
am colored and you are tiresome   I can see the great hor-
mone I give her will never take effect though it takes its toll
on me   I watch her forever and she isn't tied down but is
breathing and all the rest   I relax some soon   I shall get to
ask my question again and will demand a forthright answer
   one can expect this diligent silence to weigh heavy   does
it she speaks first dressing again in garden clothes does it
make a difference to you that I am colored   her voice as I

said is her specialty   I say it makes totally no difference first
of all because you are not colored   do you need to support
that illusion in order to maintain a relationship with me
just look at your skin in the mirrors   I see nothing in the
mirrors   you see your white skin and your pointy little nose

I am colored and I have my garden to work on   she leaves
me alone there and gloom   I almost hear the sound of war
that brought me to her garden   it is a firm relaxing sound
that puts me to sleep where I dream that I am sweating and
when I awaken I am sweating and I have the problem solved

she is swiftly building a trellis for her sugar peas   I am
colored I yell to her   she ignores me   I leap on her there in
the soft earth I am colored you see that I am colored   so she
says   so I say   so so   she doesn't look at me but begins to
cry   a little wind close to the ground lifts the dust   I am I
am colored I say as if a consolation   I thought you came to
tell me about the war   and then she bursts out wholesale
into weeping   I never know what to say if a woman cries

VI

I left her   I leave my friends their stories in my head
which of them has been lying   the air is bland   at another
end of the lake lights blow on in an elegant house though it
is midday   I am not sure that life if it were different would
be more pleasing   it is not unpleasant now and even thrill-
ing to listen to my friends   in my head he guides a new
sportscar to her door   everything I have been through col-
lides within me   he begins to tell her about the war   could
he be lying   she should have a hoe in her hand   I am happy
that she isn't home   I come back and back because she stays
out of my head though I notice that I miss her there   he is
there   he leaves with her for Texas and I follow to the ranch

of the President   she encourages him to speak to the man
about the war while she takes her swim   he tells her he
wants her by his side while he speaks to the President   she
says it makes no difference not with the President and begins
to swim   I watch her thirty laps fully dressed thirty in
panties and bra   her aquanautical prowess and general en-
durance arouse contempt in me for I can barely splash about
and usually need a motorboat   the first family watches from
the porch and they chuckle   he dives in to spend the embar-
rassing moment under water   I catch up with them again
on the prairie and beyond where New York City wavers like
a stand of poplars the air thick as jello over there   they stop
by to see Chuck who is building his own place   Chuck re-
members who she is   she is by his side and he begins to talk
about the war   where is the President   he tells the truth
and exaggerates nothing   I am bored Chuck is bored we
already know it try to forget about the war   my friends
arrive in droves before long and are pleased to meet Chuck
    she is with him   one has some food and we sit down to
eat it she has gone somewhere   my friends relax   we cour-
teously begin to lie

CHAPTER 17

Stop looking so unreal.

When we touch each other who can
say? First I sneeze (choo). We
feel, you know, kibbled. It's like
living under a wharf or in a group
of almonds.

He said, it don't even smack up.
Snack up, I replied, that's nobody's
parlance. Look before you speed
off and bludge the Great Indoors
for your forty-three compo, stilti-
fact, and omnivaraceous friends.

I divvy up with her, but she'll never
divvy. It's been ticklish these past
weeks, and nice, since I caught on
to using the group throw.

Do you think two sincere muscle-
beach people awash on the syntax
of emotion can bear the pretext of
a fork-lift? I tell you love has
chambers, thank god.

(continued on page 43) 163

5 MYTHOLOGIES

MYTHOLOGY: SAMPSON

The phony politician eyed the cruel landlord who bought off the cop but the fishy columnist was able to obscure the plot of the rotten practitioner who wiped his filthy tongs on the thigh of the oppressive strawboss's syphilitic mistress who had told the crooked dealer that the jig was up so the sly administrator could pack his embezzled fortune and board the plane which was hijacked by a sadistic colonel who had conspired with the perverted scientists that now rule the world. Tactless Sampson solved his problem by emptying his pockets. The trials of Hercules were child's play for such a nitwit as he made himself out to be. There was enough to run a store in those pockets, and he made good use of it. He only feared that someone would interrupt his reading. He preferred books, but the caustic temptress had suddenly appeared from nowhere. Had she been hired by the conspiracy of charlatans? "Yes," she said. "I am your sexpot." He lifted his arms in the nick of time and leaped from the cliff in a graceful swan dive and sliced the water like a knife through hot butter. The three intrepid hoodlums followed him on their bikes and the motors sizzled when they hit the lake. He did three hundred yards under water and came up on an enormous deserted sandy beach where there was no one to see him for miles except a huge woman in a black tank suit beneath a green awning who sucked on a leaky persimmon. She gazed out to sea. Sampson gulped and gripped the sand, fatigue rippling his massive thews. Not a thought ambled through the teeming brain. Were those voices he heard in the underbrush? Overhead enemy search planes carefully combed the area with their devil-may-care pilots. Sampson's strength slowly percolated back through his sinews. He parted the underbrush and beheld strangely painted people with awful rituals. They ate pastries. Sampson whipped out a camera and snapped a rare photo before a young brave rushed over to tell him to knock it off. Now they had him. They poked his gut with their nightsticks and tied him to a camel and dragged him to the office.

"They like to call you Sampson," said the big Prince. Slowly Sampson began to perceive where he was. It was a small yellow anteroom in a larger blue anteroom in a wing of a castle surrounded by a moat full of high-voltage eels high on a promontory overlooking a glassy plain. The man he was facing sat on a throne of nibbled balsam.

"What do you want of Sampson?" Sampson gagged. The Prince chortled and tugged a silken purple cord. Down the hall a man in kilts flipped open a latch and whispered to an inner guard who hurried down a stairway to where a stone wall could be rubbed so as to reveal a lengthy chain which a splendid Nubian could wrap around a pulley, turning it with a tremendous clank as the portcullis rose revealing a carpeted foyer in which a dark eunuch stood oiling his belly. The eunuch tiptoed over to apartment 3-A and knocked. When the woman answered he whispered to her and she immediately looked in the phone book under D. The elevator was coming fast.

"The labors of Hercules were just up your alley, you tactless nitwit," the Prince intoned.

"I always read books," Sampson wobbled a tricep.

"Well I want you should meet someone, since you're such a nice boy."

A woman entered, curtseyed, pivoted, lifted her skirts, tossed her hair back, smiled coyly, blushed like a virgin, swung her perfect hip and extended her hand that was as white as all get out.

"Sampson, I want you to meet Miss D.; Miss D., Sampson."

Goodness, Sampson thought, this is a day for déjà vu.

"*Ciao*," Miss D. murmured.

It took smelling salts to keep Sampson from passing out with desire, he found Miss D. so intoxicating.

"O.K.," said Miss D., as she leaned over him in her boudoir where the discs spun like dervishes on her turntables and her breasts smelled like cardamom. His sweetmeats were trembling. "But no French-kissing till you brush your teeth." Sampson straightened up like an icepick. Never once had he ever brushed his teeth, or anything resembling dental hygienics. "Never once have I ever brushed my teeth," he said.

The revelation hit Miss D. like a shot from the blue. "But they're stuffed with grimy, smutty gunk," she said sincerely.

Sampson gazed at her with resignation written from top to bottom. Must I reveal it again? he thought. Is a French kiss worth a power failure? Will my secret never be safe? Miss D. wriggled like a voluptuous owl.

"It's in the teeth," Sampson confessed. "That's where it is. Everything I've got in my cruddy teeth."

"You're putting me on."

"It's right there." He let loose such a filthy smile that Miss D. fell back in agony. She immediately hurried out to her unscrupulous cohorts and immediately hurried back with an uncivilized plot. She came topless to the couch of languishing Sampson. His enormous musculature quivered like a melting tabletop. She sat on his massive lap and he saw her open mouth as her face drew near and he winked as if at his buddies because he was rounding second and headed for third. Their lips plunged together and from behind her lower jaw she nudged a capsule into his mouth with her tongue. One feel of the ticklish little tip and Sampson was out. He came to in the dentist's office. "Didn't hurt," said the dentist. "Never does." Sampson swaggered to a mirror, and then paid for the cleaning at the receptionist's desk and took the abortionist's elevator to the street. It sure was refreshing. The rain stopped immediately and with the sun came a new lease on life. He took three steps at a time whenever he could.

"Sampson. Sampson," the voice of the choirboy chimed in from across the street.

"Howdy," said Sampson.

"You're just in time," said the well-trained voice.

"I always am," said Sampson, and he put his fist through the window of a nearby shop and heisted the pocket watch he had been admiring for weeks.

"Your fist is bleeding," said the voice.

"Just my hand," said Sampson.

"You were right on time," said the voice.

"Trust me," said Sampson, and he lofted the pocket watch over the huge cupola and stepped off the curb into the perpetual darkness of the endless night.

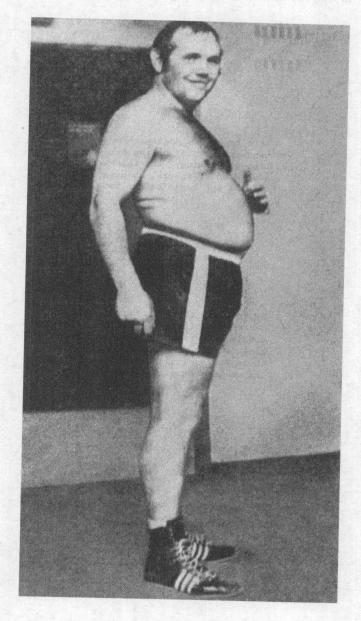

CHAPTER 1

It's enough to deal with my own
hang-ups without having her sore
lips on my mind. She thinks I'm
some kind of special Chinese
Torture put here for her benefit.

Typical was the Blue Rooster, which
became a habit in forty-three. There was
always a ferryboat captain and a
gubernatorial candidate. Yop. All
those hours sitting weren't a drop in
the bucket, holding to the outside.

 (continued on page 43)

MYTHOLOGY: POSEIDON

Poseidon was the god of the sea, which made him a wheel in his own circles, though it didn't do him any good in the water. He might better have been a float. He was up to his hubs even at the bottom. Before that he was a jockey, one of the best, until the famous third race debacle at Pimlico. That came in the third race. It was at Pimlico. Anyone who was everybody was there because they wanted to see how the god of the sea rode a horse. The sky was overcast but the track dry as the odds shifted. That was at Pimlico. They knew Poseidon's advantage on a wet track. The name of his horse was Horsh.

"Pssst," said Minnie the Wimp. They called him Minnie because he was small and always wore a kerchief around his head to hide the bald spot. "You want the sure thing on a tipped horse?" I turned around at this peculiar entreaty. "Do you mean a tip on a sure thing?" I inquired. "What do you know and how much will it cost me?" Minnie asked, pulling up closer to my mouth. At the time, my

mother didn't let me gamble, but I loved horses because
they were so pretty and had the big back. I stood up as tall
as I could to look as old as I could for as long as I could
and I said, "It looks like Poseidon on Horsh in the third."
That's how come I know this story by heart and can tell it
right off the cuff like this as if it happened to me. Minnie
gave me a dollar for the tip and I rushed out to buy a copy
of the *Partisan Review* and that's how I became a writer.
Meanwhile years passed and I left my favorite haunting
place to serve my country in the infantry where I helped
to fight the war against the Gooks. Anyone who says that
war is hell deserves a pat on the back. We went over hill
and dale looking for Gooks and when we found them we
shot them, only sometimes they found us and shot us.
They killed my best friends to the right and the left of me
right in front of my nose, and I tell you it wasn't funny. They
would have killed me too except I carried my copy of the
Partisan Review inside my jacket and the shell pierced the
Partisan Review but got only halfway to my heart. I was in
the hospital for three months where I met the nurse. She
said her name was Brett, and I laughed, so she said her
name was Brett again and I laughed again, and that was
called rest and recuperation. We climbed a mountain, we
swam in a lake, we bowled in the alley, and she wanted
me to swallow pills. It was a good thing. When it was time
for me to go back to war she said, "Put your hand right
there again." I did and she bit it. I said, "You do your bit,
Brett, and I'll go make a separate peace." She bawled and
I went back to war. It was different now because I had
no more best friends, but they killed them anyway, not
only the Gooks did it, but once our own bombers mashed
up some nearby card games. I began to understand right
then about war. It's because people don't spend enough
time at the races. If everybody spent more time at the

races they wouldn't have so much time to make war. They could win money or lose money or just sit there without killing anybody. Because if you shoot a gun and hit somebody then you hurt or kill him but if you miss then he doesn't feel it but that's what you're not supposed to do in a war because if you miss somebody then they get mad. If this sounds confused please read it again, because I got hit again soon after that in my *Partisan Review* and forgot what I was going to say because I lost my memory. When I got my memory back I noticed they had sent me home because they figure it doesn't make sense to kill a man who doesn't know who he is. You might as well kill a pineapple. So many years had passed that the old haunts seemed smaller than the new haunts. The girls looked different because they wore their hair longer whereas before they wore their hair long or else they didn't go out. I don't remember. I took a drink of well water and went back to the race track. I didn't see Minnie the Wimp because he was in the grandstand to watch the famous third race debacle which was about to begin. That was at Pimlico. I was in luck. I try not to waste any time. By then my mother didn't care if I bet or not, though she tried to make me quit smoking. I put two dollars on Horsh in the third which was ridden by Poseidon, the god of the sea, who got his start as a jockey. As I rushed to the grandstand I noticed that Minnie the Wimp was standing next to me. He told me he bet all his savings on the tip I gave him. I told him some war stories. The horses still looked pretty but their backs looked smaller. Just as it started to rain the horses were at the gate and Poseidon looked happy on Horsh. The grandstand rose to a fever pitch. As if without warning a bunch of bearded seamen appeared and tied themselves to the undersides of the horses all except for Horsh. They were off at the sound of the gun, with Horsh and Poseidon way up front, of course. Everyone was screaming for his favorite as they rounded the turn into the homestretch with men on their bellies. It was the famous third race debacle and everyone knew it. It was at Pimlico. Way out in front was Horsh, with Poseidon high on his neck, and that's how he got his famous trident, even though they disqualified him in this race. The winner was blue-eyed and cunning, and when they asked him for his name in the winner's circle this is what he said, "My name is Noman. Noman is my name." He had good timing, had long hair, and was an inspiration to the youth of tomorrow. At least Minnie the Wimp didn't lose his life savings, but Poseidon showed ambiguous sportsmanship. He took a good look at the grinning jockey and said, "Wow. What a stupid situation to get mixed up in. Let's forget it and go get a glass of retsina on the house."

CHAPTER 7

Feeling dull and lonely I swallowed
my tongue with an empty feeling and
sat in the garden among her spikes
to watch the gay bobbing chiffon at
the perimeter.

Sometimes there's an itch, but others
form a crust, for there are patches of
skin that seem to have their own
raison d'être. The least I can do is
sit by and notice with mock enthusiasm.

Lydon Johnson instigated it for his
own peace concept. He bought three
times the number of nails, the plas-
tique, and a length of twig. Okay.
The trick turned, predictably, but
too late. Nobody's heart was in it.

May you never be divulged to the passion
of ownership, and may your infants not
squander the coins of worship.

One can't be the type who will gaze at
something and say it's breezy without
having a certain conviction about clothes.
It's not Wednesday every day, by cracky.

 (continued on page 43)

MYTHOLOGY: DANAË

Danaë was so beautiful it was tough to look at her and if you looked at her it was tough to stop even though it hurt; but if you stopped she got pissed off. Nonetheless she would have been a good mother, if she hadn't fallen out with Bad Company. In fact the company wasn't expected at all, and there was nothing but carrots in the house. What could she do? The poor girl lived alone when her roommates were away, and when they were there she was usually gone. Then came a knock on the door and she wasn't there to answer it, but her roommates did and then they left. When she got back with something besides carrots she shoved the door open and there was Bad Company expecting her, so we can't blame her for the tricks of fate.

"Honey, you're such a knockout I'm afraid to look."

"Hold it," she simmered. "I'll slip into something else." She put the groceries in the hands of Bad Company and went to her boudoir to hunt up the sheerest of nylons in her armoire. She slipped her devastatingly lovely face into this mesh and rejoined Bad Company.

"You're still a sight for sore eyes," he sputtered. "But at least now I can take a gander." She let him take one and then slipped into her little apron and rushed off to putter around with dinner, and she followed the guaranteed directions on the package as a dog follows its nose to a porcupine. She split the hot-dog buns wide open. She mixed up a mixture of pure maple syrup and creamy peanut butter. She spread the mixture on the open hot-dog buns. She sprinkled the buns thickly with crispy toasted roasted flakes of wheat. She garnished the tray with radish flowers and carrot strips, opened a jar of salmon eggs, and poked the tempting treats into an oven at three hundred and forty-three degrees for three minutes till it was ready to serve with a frosted glass of something sassy or wild.

She brought it all out on a silver serving platter to find that Bad Company had split. Luckily she had made enough, and she gave them both what to eat. "Yummy," they said, and Danaë knew she had touched the heart of Bad Company. They said goodby and left without saying a word. Danaë heaved a sigh of relief and broke her roommate's sorority cup.

"That's what happens when you hang out with Bad Company," said the roommate, flashing in through the door and flashing out again with a hank of satin twine. Danaë was nonplused by that outburst, but knew the day was one. No one showed for the next two days but on the morning of the third day there was a note slid under her door that read: "No yogurt till next Friday, sorry." She wadded up that note and stuffed it down between her breasts all soft and mushroomy, then she dressed for everyday and went out in the streets. When she heard the heavy breathing at her back she whirled around to see the construction workers tearing down the housing project she lived in to make room for a new housing development. At last she was a homeless waif, ripe for the clutches of Bad Company. Try as she might to resist, she found herself drifting over to the corner lunch counter as was previously arranged, and there she ordered a regular milkshake with an egg. The counterman's eyes narrowed and he shook the shake with suspicion. Beside her sat the Awful Sequel.

"The boss has got hot rocks," he intoned through lips shut tight as two granite blocks.

"Who put the bee in his bonnet?" Danaë plunged into a well of fear.

Sequel snickered out the side of his face. "He gets what he wants when he knows what he wants if he still wants it once he gets it."

As a last line of defense, Danaë turned her fully developed front view toward him with its musky scents and the Awful Sequel clapped his mitt over his puss and fled.

The kindly counterman scooped up her dirty shake-mug and whispered, "Be on the lookout tonight. I can't say more."

Danaë walked away in good condition. She wouldn't do it. She couldn't do it. She didn't know what it was. They would never find her because it just so happened that she was a homeless waif who had no place to stay. She sat down on a park bench and thought for three hours about the advantages of poverty. At that moment she noticed that she had by chance happened to sit down on a bench across from her old home which to her chagrin was now her new home. There it was completed in the foreground. It had been quickly rebuilt, jerry-built, rejerry-built, and her roommate was waving from the window.

"Yoo-hoo, there's a somebody special here to see you."

"I'll be instantly up." She hummed a starchy tune to calm her nerves, and then rushed to her nearest house of worship to knock off a prayer. At home the prayer seemed to be answered. "It worked, by gosh," she said gleefully and dropped her wrap on the rug. "Prayer works and I believe." Then she saw the ruthless scrawl on her kitchen blackboard. EXPECT ME LATER, SNOOKS was an ominous message. She dissolved in tears and suddenly became a notorious alcoholic. She found herself in the mirror haggard and lost, and desperately trying what had worked before she slipped her face back into the sheer mesh nylon and flaked out on her sack. The boss had his own key and he sashayed into her chamber and gazed on the spectacle sprawled on the bedclothes. "A piece of gristle," he gagged. "Is this what a gangster deserves? You repay my kindness with this? What's so special about you?" Danaë popped up in the unexpected twist of events. "You're distorted," he said. "Here. Take the money and forget it."

Danaë tugged the stocking off her face quick as she could. She was really pissed off, but it was too late because The Boss had left her life forever. Now she lives a short drive from town, as predicted, and has made the wonderful mother of four boys out of herself. She wants a girl, whom she will call Phyllis. Her husband's name is Tommy, and the boys are called Harry, Martin, Joseph and Clint.

In Our Thyme *(continued from page 43)*

CHAPTER 19

They had to hire a ringer to help
heft it overboard, so that meant
risky exposure. Even so I tingled,
and then blew up.

The dried yellow rose called Linda
twitches in pigeon-down, and I like
to imitate frank happiness by sur-
rounding myself with eye-catchers.

Just because I carry my infant in
a pouch you don't have to tell me
I talk to abstract expressionists.

184 *(continued on page 43)*

MYTHOLOGY: APOLLO

"Wait till you see this beauty guy," said Iseult, as she rushed back to her chaise of pink velour, grabbed her long, inlaid cigarette holder, and poked a black Egyptian butt into the socket.

"You're such a bore with your infatuations," said Gaspara, but she nevertheless tuned up the special fluttering muscles of her thighs. Cleopatra gazed into her hand-mirror at her impeccable mascara. Marilyn puckered her special soft lips. "I don't know what you see in the type," said the one they called Ladybug who wore black lipstick and crossed her booted legs and cracked her riding crop. "All this fuss," said Brünnhilde, who sat on the edge of her couch in wheat jeans and cowboy shirt, lifting and lowering a steel ball. Jacqueline adjusted her wig.

When the door opened they all gasped, "What a beauty guy!"

Apollo was a beauty guy. He wore his hip-huggers and his striped T-shirt and his hair was curled long and golden. If it weren't for his nerves he could have been a stud. "I'm so nervous," he said. "It just isn't the same seeing you in the pictures as it is in real life and I couldn't imagine now which one to choose, I'm in such a state." A spasm of the neck jerked his head periodically and made his long curls quiver. "It's impossible," he said to Tony, the madame, and was just about to burst out in tears when he saw the little colored maid in her plain white apron cross the room with a feather duster. "Who's that?" he asked.

"Who?" Tony turned around.

Apollo lifted his hand indicating the little colored girl who was dusting the hookas, the peace pipes and syringes that surrounded the fair Baby Jane.

"You don't mean Baby Jane?" Tony warbled.

Apollo's head twitched and set his curls to springing, and he pointed again at the little colored girl.

"That one?" Tony gasped inquisitively. "Why that's just our Daphne, the little colored housegirl, who does the cleaning up in here. She's only thirteen years old. You don't want her."

"I want her."

"Well, doesn't that take the nuts out of the frosting," said Iseult, and she covered her gorgeous knees with a dishtowel. The one they called Ladybug turned to her flesh-colored hassock and beat it with the riding crop, raising scabrous red welts. Marilyn put on her glasses, picked up her volume of Meister Eckhart, and continued reading, and so it went on down the line.

Tony whispered to the little colored girl who was shaking her head slowly but resolutely. "She says she won't go," Tony related to Apollo.

"Tell her that I'm folks too," Apollo said in a rare instant of inspiration that caused a neck spasm to set his blond curls jiggling. The colored girl, when she heard this, breathed in a long colored sigh. "You aren't really," she turned and told him directly. He nodded. "You lie. You ain't folks, but you sure are a beauty guy." She took the long walk with him down the long hallway of immemorial sighs and stutters and groans. Her room was through a little door beside the broom closet, right next to the showers.

By the time they got there Apollo was twitching and jiggling like a Halloween doll, and Daphne turned to the beauty guy to say, tenderly, "Pity on you, boy. You lie in your guts when you say you're folks. Why did you have to do that? Just to get down here in the closet with Daphne? Doesn't that beat all? You're not the first one tries to catch up with me, but you're the first one caught up, and that's only because you're such a beauty guy and all those ladies of shame out there are going to be jealous like as if I had a college education, which I don't, which I ain't gonna get because it sure ain't worth much to a colored girl, but you're gonna find out that Daphne isn't much of a colored girl because she can't cook collards or black-eyed peas, never made sweet potato pie and never ate crack-lins or pork hocks. I'm just Daphne, thirteen years old and high yellow, and now you've got me, beauty guy, and I can see you don't know what to do about it, and I'm just thirteen years old and I ain't gonna give the instructions."

Apollo had never heard a protest song before and he found it refreshing. He turned white and began to whistle and his twitch was gone. She kept her eyes on him. "Beep Beep," she said. "Bang Bang." He was sweating. "Ungawa." "Enough," he said, like a prisoner of war. He figured he'd got what he wanted so he left the house of ill repute and once in the street began to hoot and wheeze and snort and stomp. Apollo was happy. He ran out and met the girl of his dreams and they got married and hustled over to the continent and found the way of the old Western world delightful as Coney Island. Then they made a lot of money. Then they had some handsome kids with loads of privileges. Then they got divorced. And then they settled down.

"Looks like the beauty guy again," Iseult of the phenomenal memory interrupted her patter with a client.

"The very one. Your very own," Apollo said, and he bowed. "And what do you know. There goes Daphne the thirteen-year-old colored girl with a feather duster. Hey there, Daphne, you pretty piece of pubescent protest."

Daphne recognized the beauty guy immediately, even though his curls had been crew-cut, and she sprinted down the hall. The paunchy Apollo lit out after her and busted the door of her room.

"Oh daddy Hudson, save me now," she wailed.

"Nothing to save you from," Apollo snickered. "I've got it all figured out now. I've had experiences with the problem. Just hold still." He reached around to grab her, but just when he touched her he felt something happen like it does in the story. She turned into a big lumpy brown leafy tree. "A magnolia," he observed. She was all hung with Spanish moss. He certainly didn't care to screw a tree so he left the room and all the girls of the house applauded him for the magnolia wreath that topped his head. He lifted it off, sniffed it, and tossed it to them; then he set his jaw and shoulders, and stepped into the street, and lo and behold: the city was on fire.

CHAPTER 13

I told you mixed fry and not
steamed pudding. Your wish-
ful thinking could mean death
for thousands. Next time pay
attention and accept gifts.

She faltered at the oatmeal
and looked up. "Turgid."
There was someone mysterious
who had snowed on her scorched
earth policy.

 (continued on page 43)

MYTHOLOGY: HOMER

Homer was a writer par excellence. He could write in mid-stream where others would have to paddle. He could write spread-eagled or upside down or skinning the cat. He could write a poem with both eyes shut. He could write like the wind. He was an all-around writer of the old school, with a pinch of the new school thrown in. The kids wrote in his senior yearbook that here was a man who was supposed to be top rung. The writings he wrote in his teens would shame a man in his twenties. Almost at the drop of a bucket he wrote ten books. Their titles were: FRIED CUCUMBERS, BUTCHERED CARROTS, PRESSED WEENIES, WATERED ALMONDS, BOILED PERSIMMONS, TORTURED MUSH, MIXED CHOPS, FAITHFUL OKRA, RINSED MELONS, and THANKS. He wrote so fast he hardly had time to help himself until he suddenly noticed that all the editors were saying, "No dice," and he realized it was up to him, so he printed up seven thousand copies of a book he called THREE SQUARE MEALS A DAY LEADS TO HAPPINESS AND

HEALTH WITH OTHER STORIES, but they all burned up in a distillery fire, except for the one his Uncle Ted stole. The writings Homer wrote in his twenties would shame a man in his thirties. Soon all the editors sat up and took notice, and they accepted a brand new novel of his called CRUNCHY. Unfortunately he left the manuscript in a briefcase on a train and never found out where it got off. The editors decided that his reconstruction of the manuscript had no zest and canceled his contract and in that period he wrote his two gloomiest books: SPUN SUGAR and FLAKES OVER THE ORANGE PIT. At the former the editors turned up their noses, and they said thumbs down to the latter. Homer decided then he was running out of luck, and his case was the one on which the new regulation about writers is based, that the law immediately publish the first three books of any new writer until he turns famous and relaxes; then he is told to improve. Homer might have been born too soon, but the writings he wrote in his thirties would shame a man in his forties. Too bad he had to become a daredevil pilot.

As a pilot he was a real daredevil because he couldn't figure how to navigate. Words were his specialty and he didn't know many numbers. South south east suggested to him the titles of three new novels which were called LOQUAT, THE NOISE OF THE PRICKLY PEAR, and TAP ON THE MAPLE, and he wouldn't put the plane down anywhere till the three books were thoroughly mapped out in his brain. That made him a daredevil pilot, especially when he landed blind on the enemy landing strip in the midst of confusion and was hustled immediately to headquarters, where he swiped a ream of paper and started to write. He never looked up once despite the vicious threats, but through thick and thin got well into the second narrative by the time the air strip fell back into friendly hands that all applauded him, but it was too late because the enemy had already swiped the manuscript and they published it immediately, disguised under the title of SMALL FRUIT. Homer, flushed by sudden success, defected immediately, but you have to realize that the writings he wrote in his forties would shame a man in his fifties. After he learned the new language and understood that for them he would have to write books like POTATO, SOUP, CARROT, BREAD, he realized that the enemy wasn't his bag and stowed away on a freighter to a little South Sea island where he lived for many years without a care in the world among brownish folks who couldn't read. He scraped his stories on the rocks and carved them on the trees. There was where he invented the characters for which he is most beloved today: Blotio, Mercopaylayadine, and everybody's favorite, Ellipsedos. Many of us have passages from the sublime ELLIPSIDOTE by heart these days: "Spurning the leaden wave-crush they planted their oars like onion sets in the loamy sea, and plugged in to the purple night of Starnadine to once in the end confront the blushing Terror of the Deep. The hearts of the men were heavy as pan bread when the woman turns her back on the oven and lets the dough sit too long, causing it to fall again, so it won't rise in the baking, in the pan, to produce the light fluffy crusts of bread for which the islanders are notorious, for which they lick their chops." Passages like these, so rich in tender figures, in the peculiar metabolic metaphor such as "blushing terror" typical of the middle late Homer, and the last remarkable extension of image where his genius runs rampant, combining the emotions of men with old-fashioned home cooking are what we love him best for and is why we say that the things he wrote in his fifties would shame a man in his sixties. The life of utter pleasure paled on him after a time so he decided to head for home where he could settle the old scores. He found there that a younger generation was entrenched writing new novels called BUST THE FROZEN SPINACH, COUNT-DOWN TO GRAPEFRUIT and ELECTRONIC LEMON PUCKER, exhibiting evidence of his influence, though his work was unknown to the people. He got the cold shoulder when he asked around what was up because he was such an old-timer, except for Mary True who fell in love with him though she was only seventeen. She went to live with him in a Styrofoam hut on the beach while he wrote his penultimate oeuvre which he called BLUE FIGS BLACK FIGS YELLOW FIGS PINK FIGS MAUVE FIGS GREEN FIGS PUCE FIGS OCHRE FIGS AND THE PORTABLE CHAIN SAW. Every-body sat up and took notice and embarrassed Mary True, who left him for a dock worker, breaking his heart and shearing ten years off his life. She now lives with two weight lifters in Spokane. With his final, most complex, most revealing and least palatable book, LURD CHOMP, he became a beloved author, and we say of him today that the things he wrote in his seventies would shame a man in his twenty-fives.

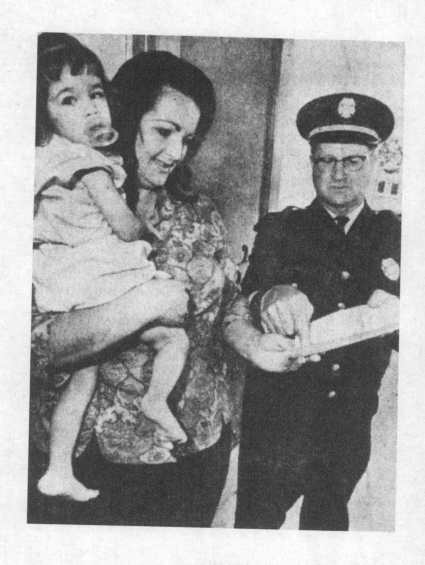

CHAPTER 4

Last time there was a glimpse
of foolishness, a trapped look,
a modest twitch, but since then
my features have set.

Each day we lunched together and
the noise deteriorated until per-
fection was in our grips. Suddenly
she jumped into bed with me. You
call us fortunate? There were
still seven of us to whistle.

BLOSSOMS

Tap. Tap Tap Tap Tap Tap. Tap Tap. Tap Tap. I make that sound before I come through the wall. You are forewarned. There she stood with her soft knit hat topping her head, and I noted in her eyes that dark finished look, like calmed water. It was clear that for her the argument was over before it had begun for me. I decided to say anything. "You're lucky to have those hands." Her fingers were slender and wide apart and strong and paint-spotted. I couldn't remember that she didn't know who I was. My center wanted her and my left shoulder and my left cheekbone. Not a chance. I needed some sense of how she felt about everything, but her silence was sending me away. My middle rose up and asked permission to speak, but it was too late. I left. Now I shall need some help with this story.

That was a mushy curtain-raiser which hardly fore-shadows what follows. On the next day the insurrection blinded one of us to the other, and even to the violence of insurrection. You are probably curious, nonetheless, of how I got into this basket to have my arms and legs lopped off and my eyes destroyed. Well, you are mistaken. The story isn't even a long one. I still walk around. MARTIN LUTHER KING IS SLAIN. But I won't go near a basket unless to disguise my intention, which right now is to let you think that everything is hunky-dory. I'll make the facts exert themselves.

Our task was to seek the cache of defectors, insinuate into their zone, reveal unto them, lay down some posh alternatives, and then triumph. Each of us moved at a different speed, and when I saw us fanned out across the meadow I felt special. We were synchronized to arrive simultaneously so that what looked like a ragtag bunch of misfits would coalesce into a vital action group. Mr. Ledbetter put his ear to the ground, his transistor to the other ear, his finger in the other ear, tuned in on "Even the Bad Times Are Good," La la lalala laa laa Laaa Laaa wafting over the freshly devastated meadow. What he heard is top secret. There seemed to be no opposition, on a perfect evening, the smoggy sky like a lavender skirt. We arrived within seconds, and though the target was mistaken the mission happened to be a success. Phase two was up. Just then my own man friday, called Henry David Thoreau, dropped a blockbuster. "I want out," he said. He was irreplaceable.

"Can't you wait, Hank, until . . ." I faltered because he looked so solid and intransigent. "Can't you . . ."

"I decided it was the last time I would come across the meadow, across that fucking lie. My heart's full up: If I count to ten will you look around at what's really happening?"

Though I agreed with him, it was still my job to keep the outfit together. I said, "Hank. Hank. Hank. Hank. Hank. Hank. Slow down your mind and try to remember how in the first place we got started, you did, but we together, you first, me too. What was important when we began? Our purpose is long and grim but we can't falter now, or else what will they say?" He took off one of his hands at the wrist and gave it to me. "Now. Now." I tried to shake a desperate sound into my voice. "Now is the time for unflagging will, for a coordinated effort." I was full of shit, and I knew it. I had no idea what I was saying and I said it without conviction, and he could smell it. It was time to lay some names on my vague argument. "Hank, things were dark at Blyville. Things were black at Barge Valley. Pony's Thumb was a near disaster." One of his arms came off in my hand and he gave me his nose. "You were with me in Port Martha. We were together . . ." I was embarrassed to stand there holding his stuff in front of all the others. He turned in his other arm.

"I wish you could explain to me why I should continue to be a part of this insane risky process of totally guiltless fiendishness. One reason you believe in yourself. Do you remember a cause you once had, you still have. I still like you, my friend." As he spoke he loosened a leg at the knee.

"Friendship is a reason, Hank."

"Friendship is a dispute with reason. You don't march into, excuse the expression, hell, just to please your friend. If you, out of this confusion, can explain to me what at all we are doing, I can perhaps tell you if I agree with it or not." He slowly continued his self-dismemberment, laying a foot, a calf, a thigh into the cradle of my extended arms.

"We're doing what we're doing," I said, receiving the lower half of his torso on top of the pile of limbs.

"Don't you ever look around at the damage we've done?" He deposited his thorax part on my arms.

"You know as well as I do, Hank, that I was meant to spend my time with beautiful women. Of course I look around, and I don't like what I see, but it's the times, these times. What can we do? The times conspire with itself to make meatballs of men."

The last part he gave me was the head, partially disassembled, eyes and cheeks and teeth hanging loose. His final gesture, one so indecorous I still don't understand it, low and childish, was to dislodge the genitalia, and cork the mouth with his own partly erected cock. "There," he said. "Now I've returned all the equipment I borrowed. Goodby." He left. I was numbed. There in my arms I held all the parts of Henry David Thoreau.

"You see what he left me? You see what I've got now?" The others looked away. I was crying. They were itching for phase two. I left the parts in a heap where I stood, and perhaps they are still there. We paired off for the second phase, to scour the great indoors; the gray wallpaper with huge purple flowers, the wicker rocking chair, the stub of a cheroot, four seed catalogs, the Book of Mormon—not a defector to be had in this environment. How we thirsted at that moment for a nub of success.

Most of the day improved on itself, however. You see, I met her on that day, O predictions of Zakamondo. All afternoon my timepiece languished at four pee em. She was still waiting for a bus, sweet innocent, unaware that those vehicles too had been appropriated. There was beauty, waste and phosphorescence about her gestures, so I picked her up in my staff car and I loved her, my God, I confessed everything, turned it all over to her, and my body is puny with anticipation, without hope. Though throngs of luscious women press on my forehead, she boots them away. She has a powerhouse in her ankles. I'll never find out what all this means. It's the times have blurred the connections, but I still want to make something terribly clear.

At four pee em the bombs began to bang around us, surprising no one. Nobody's desperate any more, just numb. The air has a familiar smell, but with our faces in it we smell the soil. Were we cautious enough? Each man frequently mentions his own life.

"Over here. Here, Here." A familiar voice beckoned from

a hole. What a surprise. The head poking out was of my favorite grad-school companion, John Quincy Adams, and he had a tunnel. "Halloooo," I cried. "Quince, could that be you?" We crawled there on our bellies, those of us who had them. All the defectors were down there in the tunnel, and they had been abandoned, so we could glide through the assignment, each one a soft kill. The last was my dear old friend John Quincy Adams and he said, "It's so exasperating to spend five hours on a problem and get just nowhere, just to have it prop . . ." We sliced his windpipe. End assignment. Now I have come to the moral of all this.

It probably crossed the minds of each of you that this author is perverse to make "Blossoms" a title for his story. Tap. Where do blossoms ever enter? If so, are they blossoms? Tap Tap Tap Tap Tap. Here's a likely place, and if I'm wrong may you eat my words. Tap Tap. I will fill these pages with blossoms, and even before I begin I need to put this confession up to you, that I'm not actually a human type. Tap Tap. You probably didn't suspect it, but I'm a pet dog.

Chamomile blossoms, petunia blossoms, lavender blossoms, rose blossoms, tulip blossoms, adder's-tongue blossoms, hyacinth blossoms, jonquil blossoms, sweetbriar blossoms, bloodroot blossoms, lilac blossoms, Dutchman's-breeches blossoms, lemon blossoms, jack-in-the-pulpit blossoms, forsythia blossoms, cornflower blossoms, azalea blossoms, no fig blossoms, prickly-pear blossoms, daffodil blossoms, dogwood blossoms, squash blossoms, sweat-pea blossoms, Eucalyptus blossoms. something seriously ain't coming across here. lady's-slipper blossoms, morning-glory blossoms, trillium blossoms, bachelor's-button blossoms, ragweed blossoms, heather blossoms, carnation blossoms, iris blossoms, chaparral blossoms or snowbrush blossoms, yucca blossoms, rocklily blossoms, Joshua blossoms, fennel blossoms, wisteria blossoms, Eucalyptus blossoms, bougainvillea blossoms, poppy blossoms, mint blossoms, choho blossoms, perny blossoms, sharja blossoms, calish blossoms, histox blossoms. The point will never stray across this way. Let's back it up.

Self blossoms. Flesh blossoms. War blossoms. Stumble blossoms. Cherry blossoms Cherry blossoms. Fall blossoms. Ink blossoms. Tactic blossoms. Napalm blossoms. Top blossoms. Scorch blossoms. Lazy-dog blossoms. Cherry blossoms. Glory blossoms. Cherry blossoms. Flag blossoms. Cherry blossoms. Commander blossoms. Assault blossoms. Flame blossoms. Pursue blossoms. Brass blossoms. Deal blossoms. Cherry blossoms. Cherry blossoms.

These blossoms. I like to walk in them when they are blossoms. Often I crush them when I walk and the sweetest odor seeps up the foot that asks you to sit down though it's perilous. I called Chuck, my friend, to see if he wanted to risk a walk in blossoms. He wasn't. He took his chances for mushrooms, not for blossoms, he took it for mushrooms. No way to argue that point, but I leaned to blossoms just the same. I was out. They were fine, big-hued bushfuls of them that made you tremble. I learned color. I learned scent. I learned sky. I learned cloud in sky. Most of all bravery. Blossom is bravery in my economy. I stood in the tomato-red field of endless small poppies, and there with its roots dipped in sulfur-yellow dandelion blossom was the blossomless and ancient olive tree. How was I possessed? I walked over to that tree and sat down in yellow at its roots, and snoozed. I can't tell if I had a dream or not; perhaps, but I woke up scared. What foolishness. Foolish blossoms. My palms were sweaty. I hustled back to see her, dodging the fateful blossoms. Could her studio have been empty? The easel held a still life of twelve apples, eight plums, sixteen lemons, a peeled red banana, and a pink vase topped with a watermelon in which she had sunk her palette knife. She was lying on the bed, breathing often, but buried head to toe in nondescript blossoms. Neither of us spoke. I lifted the blossoms off her precious flesh where they left their pastel stains. Some were plastic blossoms. I offer those to you, reader, who won't wait for the fruit. Forgive us again, and patience. For you these blossoms in the presence of your own ambition. Forgive me. I leave you blossoms. In the bad times, or the worst, these blossoms.

CHAPTER 22

Angry? You can't believe the
tête-à-tête. You do an orange
with a fine edge and it can't turn
out otherwise, so who's finicky?

 (continued on page 43)

Others just doze and smoke and dream away the day . . .

STEVE KATZ IN BRIEF

STEVE KATZ was born at The Bronx on May 14, 1935. Just
then his family moved to Manhattan, to Washington Heights,
where he attended Public School 173 and Humboldt Junior
High School. He played baseball in Jayhood Wright Park,
and basketball in The Schoolyard. At age nine he had his
first taste of pizza. He was a founding member of the New
York Bullets social and athletic club and sported their
purple and gold reversible jacket. He has flown kites and
has ridden sleds. When Steve Katz was fifteen a kid stabbed
his basketball with a stiletto. One year later he was sixteen.

ABOUT THE AUTHOR

Steve Katz (1935–2019) was an American post-modern/avant-garde writer. He received his bachelor of arts degree from Cornell University in 1956 and his master of arts degree from the University of Oregon in 1959. He taught creative writing at the English Language Institute and the University of Maryland Overseas (both in Italy), Cornell University, the University of Iowa, Brooklyn College, Queens College, and Notre Dame University. In 1978, he became Director of Creative Writing at the University of Colorado, Boulder. Katz was the recipient of two National Endowment for the Arts grants (1976 and 1981), and a Creative Artists Public Service grant (1976). Has also worked for the Forest Service in Idaho, in a quicksilver mine in Nevada, and on dairy farms in New York State. He started teaching Tai Chi Chuan in1971.

At Cornell in the 1950s, Katz encountered Vladimir Nabokov and Thomas Pynchon, and later roomed at the Chelsea Hotel in Manhattan where he met Janis Joplin, Andy Warhol, John Ashbery, George Plimpton, Kurt Vonnegut, Jr., Philip Glass, and countless other artists and scenesters of the 1960s and '70s.

Literary critic Jerome Klinkowitz wrote that Katz has "pushed innovation farther than any of his contemporaries," and W. C. Bamburger dubbed him "the most important living American novelist." (*43 Views of Steve Katz, Popular Writers of Today*, vol. 69, Borgo Press, 2007)

ACKNOWLEDGMENTS

The publisher extends his profound thanks to the following for their generous financial support which helped to defray some of this edition's production costs:

Kevin Adams, Dennys Antunish, Mark Axelrod-Sokolov,
Thomas Young Barmore Jr, Kian S. Bergstrom,
Brad Bigelow (neglectedbooks.com), Blister Four Eyes,
Matthew Boe, Brian R. Boisvert, Bonriguez,
Giacomo Boschelle, Jordan Brodeur, Chris Call,
Captain Awesome, Sebastian Castillo, Scott Chiddister,
Joel Coblentz, Daniel Cockrell, G Cooperman, Sheri Costa,
Parker & Malcolm Curtis, Frank Derfield Jr.,
Dylan & Sam Doomwarre, James Duncan, Isaac Ehrlich,
Dayna Epley, Pops Feibel, Keith Forsyth, Tom Foster,
Jesse James Fox, Justin Gallant, Pierino Gattei,
Stephan Glander, GMarkC, J Godwin, Gary Goff,
B F Gordon Jr & R Katz, Erik G. C. Hemming, Aric Herzog,
J. Holmes, Hall Hood, Haya K., Gautham Kalva,
Rebekah Kass, David Kenny, Stefan Kruger, Ray Kutch,
Kyle, Mark Lamb, Jean-Jacques Larrea, Dana West Lawlor,
Ty Lechtenberg, Giles Leonard, Ben Lieberman,
Gardner Linn, Nick Long, T. Lucas,
Brian de León Macchiarelli, Jonathan Mack, Marcel,
Jim McElroy, Donald McGowan, BT McMenomy,
Jack Mearns, William J. Mego,
Dr. Melvin "Steve" Mesophagus, Jason Miller,
Spencer F Montgomery, Geoffrey Moses,
Gregory Moses, T. Motley, Scott Murphy,
Séamus Murphy, Clyde Nads, Anthony Notaro,
Matt O'Connell, Michael O'Shaughnessy, Nick Oxford,

Luis Panini, Andrew Pearson, Pedro Ponce, Stephen Press,
Ned Raggett, Judith Redding, Ryan C. Reeves,
Patrick M Regner, Daniel Rhine, Steven Rineer, Rebecca S,
George Salis (www.TheCollidescope.com),
Frank V. Saltarelli, Christopher H. Sartisohn,
Tiffany Schademan, Bjoern Roland Schnabel, Don Schulz,
Kelly Snyder, Yvonne Solomon, K. L. Stokes, Tousedsa,
Christopher Wheeling, Isaiah Whisner, Karl Wieser,
Charles Wilkins, John Wirkner, Brad Wojak, T.R. Wolfe,
the Zemenides family, and Anonymous